"Tonight I intend to go to bed with my fiancée."

In a panic, Fran cried, "No! I've done as you asked so far. I've taken Melinda's place at the party. But I've no intention of taking her place in your bed. I *won't* be a substitute—"

"Who said anything about a substitute?" Blaze broke in coldly. "In any case, you'll be anything I want you to be. As I pointed out earlier this evening, you owe me...."

"Don't force me to sleep with you," she begged.

"You know as well as I do that there won't be any need for force. Sexually we always struck sparks off each other."

LEE WILKINSON lives with her husband in a three-hundred-year-old stone cottage in an English village, which most winters gets cut off by snow. They both enjoy traveling and have previously joined forces with their daughter and son-in-law, spending a year going around the world "on a shoestring" while their son looked after Kelly, their much-loved German shepherd dog. Her hobbies are reading and gardening and holding impromptu barbecues for her long-suffering family and friends.

Books by Lee Wilkinson

HARLEQUIN PRESENTS®
1933—THE SECRET MOTHER
1991—A HUSBAND'S REVENGE
2024—WEDDING FEVER
2107—THE MARRIAGE TAKEOVER

Don't miss any of our special offers. Write to us at the following address for information on our newest releases.

Harlequin Reader Service
U.S.: 3010 Walden Ave., P.O. Box 1325, Buffalo, NY 14269
Canadian: P.O. Box 609, Fort Erie, Ont. L2A 5X3

Lee Wilkinson

SUBSTITUTE FIANCÉE

ISBN 0-373-12154-9

SUBSTITUTE FIANCÉE

First North American Publication 2001

Copyright © 2000 by Lee Wilkinson

All rights reserved. Except for use in any review, the reproduction or utilization of this work in whole or in part in any form by any electronic, mechanical or other means, now known or hereafter invented, including xerography, photocopying and recording, or in any information storage or retrieval system, is forbidden without the written permission of the publisher, Harlequin Enterprises Limited, 225 Duncan Mill Road, Don Mills, Ontario, Canada M3B 3K9.

All characters in this book have no existence outside the imagination of the author and have no relation whatsoever to anyone bearing the same name or names. They are not even distantly inspired by any individual known or unknown to the author, and all the incidents are pure invention.

This edition published by arrangement with Harlequin Books S.A.

HARLEQUIN®

TORONTO • NEW YORK • LONDON
AMSTERDAM • PARIS • SYDNEY • HAMBURG
STOCKHOLM • ATHENS • TOKYO • MILAN • MADRID
PRAGUE • WARSAW • BUDAPEST • AUCKLAND

ISBN 0-373-12154-7

SUBSTITUTE FIANCÉE

First North American Publication 2001.

Copyright © 2000 by Lee Wilkinson.

CHAPTER ONE

FRANCESCA HOLT, making her way through the Friday afternoon press of people and luggage-piled trolleys, paused to glance up at the airport's flight monitors.

The plane from Amsterdam had just landed. She breathed a sigh of relief.

'Really it's a damned nuisance having to go away just now,' Kirk had said. 'But this trip is far too important to cancel.'

He'd kissed her and picked up his bag and briefcase. 'I'll be back tomorrow without fail. Meet me by the main reception desk. There's only twenty minutes or so between our planes, so you won't have long to wait.' With a teasing smile, he'd added, 'Just keep a tight hold on your handbag until I join you.'

Taking up a position within sight of the reception desk, she waited quietly.

She was a slim, graceful woman, of above medium height, with silky ash-brown hair, which had a slight tendency to curl, twisted into a knot on top of her head.

She was dressed nicely, if unadventurously, in a silky oatmeal-coloured dress with self-buttons, and a short, collarless jacket. A flimsy flowered scarf around her throat added a touch of colour. She carried a small weekend case and a handbag.

Unexceptional, the man watching her thought, apart from a lovely figure and a certain quality of stillness that made her stand out from the crowd.

Serenely unaware that she was under surveillance, Fran lifted her left hand and glanced at the small diamond solitaire she wore. Kirk had slipped it on to her finger just a couple of nights ago, when he'd taken her out to dinner.

'This is only temporary,' he'd told her. 'You can choose something bigger and better when this coming weekend's over.'

But she didn't need anything bigger and better. Engaged to the blue-eyed, golden-haired Mr Wonderful of most women's fantasies, she had everything she wanted.

As well as film star good looks, Kirk had a quick intelligence and loads of charm, a 'way with him' that was irresistible.

When she had moved to the Midlands to take up a post as designer for Christopher Varley—a reputable and long-established Manchester firm of goldsmiths and jewellers—Kirk Varley, son of the late owner, had treated her with the same casual friendliness he reserved for all his other employees.

Even after almost a year, and growing success as several of her imaginative designs had attracted a good deal of attention, he had shown no sign of interest.

Then a commission to redesign an antique necklace had worked the miracle.

Kirk had been approached by Edward Balantyne, a multi-millionaire businessman and owner of Balantyne Hall, who'd wanted his bride to wear the necklace at their wedding.

Made up of eighteen large, perfectly matched rubies, it was reputed to have been given to Elizabeth Balantyne, a noted beauty, by an Indian maharaja in the early days of the Raj.

Since then a Balantyne family tradition had grown up, so that with each generation the necklace was passed on to the eldest son's bride.

But this time, unimpressed by its history and disliking its heavy, old-fashioned appearance, the American bride-to-be, having seen and admired Francesca's work, wanted the priceless gems put into a lighter, modern setting.

Needing to be in the States for the few weeks prior to his wedding, the multi-millionaire, apparently with some reluctance, had finally agreed to allow his fiancée a free hand in choosing the new design.

Before leaving, and after reaching an agreement with Kirk, Edward Balantyne had made arrangements for the necklace to be taken by special security from his London bank to the jewellers.

It would arrive just twenty-four hours before William Bailey, the firm's craftsman, was due to reset the rubies, and Varleys would be responsible for handing it back safely.

There had been one stipulation. Having in the past been hounded by the media on both sides of the Atlantic, Edward Balantyne had insisted that the whole thing, including his forthcoming marriage, which was to take place in London shortly after his return from the States, should remain a closely guarded secret.

'I can understand why,' Kirk had said. 'Apart from the security angle, he's marrying Melinda, the daughter of Gideon Ross. If the press found out, they'd have a field-day.

'Ross was recently mixed up in some Wall Street embezzlement scandal that made front page news even in England. He ended up disgraced and penniless, and was lucky to escape prison.'

Determined to take no chances on Edward Balantyne's secret getting out, Kirk had arranged for Melinda Ross, a gorgeous blonde, to meet Fran and himself at a quiet Manchester hotel, rather than his business premises.

That first discussion, with a life-sized photograph of the necklace and precise measurements, had been followed by a series of lunchtime meetings, during which the bride-to-be had looked at several of Fran's designs and chosen the one she liked best.

Listening to Fran's ideas, and getting to know her as a woman, rather than simply an employee, had sparked Kirk's interest, and he had started to wine and dine her.

Now, only a short time later, he had suggested she move in with him while they made preparations for a spring wedding.

In love, and reassured by the word *wedding*, she had—for the first time since Blaze—let down her defences and agreed.

Kirk, his blond good looks the antithesis of Blaze's darkly handsome face—a face she still couldn't think of without her heart turning over—had looked both pleased and relieved.

He had helped her transport her few personal possessions to his sumptuous apartment just before she'd seen him off at the airport.

'It's your home now,' he'd said, smiling. 'You can move in as soon as you like.'

But, unwilling to actually take up residence before his return, Fran had refused a key and stayed where she was, only handing in the keys of her own rented flat that morning.

Now she warmed herself with the thought that when the weekend was over she and Kirk would be going home together, and a new and happier phase in her life would be starting...

A slight smile hanging on her lips, she glanced up and met the eyes of a thin, sharp-faced man with sandy hair, who appeared to be watching her.

Without conscious volition Fran's hand went to her throat, but already the man was turning away.

Though he looked ordinary enough there was something vaguely familiar about the stooped shoulders, the creased suit and, rather incongruously, the mac over his arm.

Surely he'd been on the same Manchester to London plane as herself?

Seeing him wander in the direction of the flight monitors, she relaxed. Like herself, he was probably waiting for someone.

A glance at her watch confirmed that Kirk should be with her any minute, and she breathed a sign of relief. She would be glad when they reached Balantyne Hall and this whole thing was over.

'Don't be silly,' he'd said briefly, when she'd first baulked at his idea. 'As we're going to the Hall, it's the perfect solution.'

'Surely it would be safer to let the security firm deliver it?' she pleaded.

'Not necessarily.'

Seeing she wasn't convinced, he admitted, 'And there's another consideration. Trade hasn't been up to much for the past year or so, and special security costs a great deal of money, which would have to come out of our profits.'

But she considered it too big a responsibility to be part of such a plan, and said so. 'After all I'm only an employee...'

'My darling girl...' He drew her into his arms. 'You must know that I don't think of you as a mere employee. In fact I was about to ask you to become part of the firm.'

As she stared at him, wondering if she'd misunderstood, he smiled. 'Yes, I really *do* mean marry me...'

After an interval of kisses and whispered endearments, he added purposefully, 'As for the necklace; I can assure you there's absolutely no risk involved.'

'But if Mr Balantyne's expecting it to be delivered by Rayburns won't he—?'

A shade impatiently, Kirk broke in, 'So long as it's returned *safely*, it's up to us. Look, if I think there's likely to be a problem, I'll clear it with him. But really it makes a lot of sense to do it this way.

'The whole thing's been worked with such secrecy that apart from William Bailey—and he's as safe as houses—there's not a soul knows we've ever had the necklace in our possession.

'Now, don't worry any more. For one thing, Balantyne is sure to have it insured up to the hilt... You just meet me at the airport and we'll be home and dry. Nothing can go wrong.

'A taxi should get us to Balantyne Hall by late afternoon. There'll be plenty of time to talk to our host and hostess and get business over before dinner.

'So far as I know, there'll only be the four of us on Friday night; the actual party isn't until Saturday...'

To coincide with the delivery of the necklace, Edward Balantyne was planning to hold an engagement party to introduce his bride-to-be to his family and a few close friends.

The invitation to Kirk and herself to attend the party and spend the weekend at his ancestral home had come as a surprise.

To Fran's way of thinking, it was not a particularly pleasant one. Neither of them had actually met Edward Balantyne, and what she'd heard about him from Melinda Ross hadn't made a good impression.

Still, Kirk had seemed pleased and oddly excited by the invitation...

But where on earth *was* Kirk? Surely he should be here by now?

'Will Miss Holt, meeting Mr Varley, please go to the reception desk...?' The disembodied voice broke into her thoughts.

Feeling a quiver of apprehension, Fran crossed to the desk and identified herself.

'There's a message for you, Miss Holt.' The woman behind the desk was briskly efficient and impersonal. 'Mr

Varley has been unavoidably delayed. He wants you to proceed to the Hall, where he'll join you as soon as possible.'

'He didn't have any idea how long he'd be?'

'Apparently not.'

'Thank you.' Clutching her case and shoulder-bag, Fran turned away, beset by a sudden surge of something close to panic.

Taking a deep breath, she told herself not to be a fool. Apart from the fact that she would have to make the journey to Balantyne Hall alone, nothing had really altered.

All she had to do was get a taxi.

Avoiding a milling crowd of pink and peeling holiday-makers, struggling with bags and packages and recalcitrant children, she made her way to the exit.

Outside, the September heat, trapped between the buildings, was sweltering, and the air seemed curiously heavy and stale.

The pavement was crowded with people and trolleys, the roadway noisy with cars and vehicles picking up passengers and loading luggage.

A straggling queue of people waited at the taxi rank. Several taxis appeared together, and the queue in front of her diminished, leaving Fran at the head.

Another taxi pulled into the kerb. As she stepped forward to open the door her handbag was snatched from her, and a violent sideways push sent her sprawling.

Shocked and dazed, she struggled to her knees, and a moment later was being helped to her feet by a silver-haired man standing behind her in the queue.

The whole thing had been over in a split second, most of the crowd seeming unaware of what had happened.

'Are you all right?' The man, who with his neatly trimmed moustache and a military air looked like a retired colonel, stooped to pick up her case.

A hand to her throat, she croaked, 'I'm fine. Just a bit

shaken.' Recognising him as a fellow passenger on the Manchester flight, she managed a smile.

'Would you like me to call Airport Security?'

'No, I don't think so,' Fran refused hastily. 'I need to get on.' The last thing she wanted was to be held up for ages.

'You really should tell the police,' the 'colonel' insisted.

'I'm sure you're right. I'll report it later.' Taking her case, she thanked him and scrambled into the taxi.

By the time she'd given the driver the address, shock had set in and she was trembling in every limb.

Gritting her teeth, she made an effort to pull herself together while she inspected the damage. A grazed palm and bleeding knees, torn tights, smears of dust on her dress and jacket and scuffed shoes seemed to be all.

No doubt there would be bruises later, but, taking everything into consideration, she had got off lightly.

The big question in her mind was, why had the thief picked on her? Could he have known who she was, or had any inkling of Kirk's plan?

No, surely not. This was small-time theft. There were dozens of such crimes each day. It must be sheer coincidence that she had been a target.

A strange and bizarre coincidence, nevertheless...

Fran shivered. Then, shrugging off a feeling of nameless apprehension, she brought her mind back to the present and glanced out of the window.

After leaving the airport environs behind them they had reached leafy country roads which carried comparatively little traffic.

In a mile or so, shortly after passing a pleasantly rustic hotel, they turned left, past a magnificent stand of beeches just starting to turn gold, and began to follow an old lichen-covered stone wall.

Before long they came to a pair of black ornamental wrought-iron gates, flanked by stone pillars.

'This is Balantyne Hall,' the taxi driver advised her, drawing to a halt.

Looking at the gates, which didn't appear to open, she asked, 'Are you sure this is the right entrance?'

'We can use this one, though it's not the main entrance. That's about a mile further on and has a manned gatehouse. As it happens I've been here before... There's a sort of intercom system on all the gates, if you'd like to tell me your name?'

She told him.

Leaving the engine running, he went over to a panel in the gates and, having pressed a button, spoke into a small grille.

Lifting her eyes, Fran noticed a high-up security camera scanning the entrance. It seemed Edward Balantyne didn't take any chances.

The driver climbed back into the cab and the gates slid aside to allow them entry, before closing silently after them.

They followed the well-kept drive, which was bordered by flowering plants and shrubs, until they rounded the curve of a low hill and the house came into view.

Low and rambling, with creeper-covered walls built of mellow stone, it had mullioned windows, twisted barley-sugar chimneys and a hotchpotch of crooked roofs and gables.

Fran drew a breath of surprise and delight. She had expected something large and square and imposing, rather than this charming old manor-house nestling like a contented babe in the warm sunshine.

When the taxi came to a stop on the paved apron, Fran picked up her case and was in the act of stepping out when it came home to her that she had no money to pay the driver.

Feeling foolish, she realised that her only option was to ask him to wait while she rang the bell, explained the situation, and borrowed some.

At that instant the door of the house opened and a dignified black-coated butler appeared. Tall and spare, with a lugubrious face and greying hair slicked straight back, he could have been any age between forty and sixty.

Never having seen a real-life butler before, Fran was duly impressed.

She was about to explain her predicament when he went over to the cab and handed some notes to the driver, who thanked him and drove away.

Of course, the call from the gates had warned of her arrival, but how had anyone known she would need the taxi fare?

Showing no sign of surprise at her dishevelled state, the butler said gravely, 'Allow me, miss.' Relieving her of her case, he led the way into a long oak-panelled hall. 'If you'll follow me, miss, I'll show you to your room.'

As they mounted the beautifully carved staircase he added, 'The master considered that you might appreciate a few minutes to tidy up, before joining him in the living room for some tea.'

Fran wondered if 'the master' had extra-sensory perception. It was almost as if he was aware of what had happened without her needing to explain a thing.

Crossing the landing, the butler opened a door to the left and, having placed her case on what appeared to be an Elizabethan sea-chest, informed her, 'You'll find the living room at the far end of the hall, miss.'

She smiled at him. 'Thank you, er...'

'Mortimer, miss.'

'Thank you, Mortimer.'

With a half-bow, the stately figure departed.

Her room was white-walled and simple, with a wide stone fireplace and polished oak floorboards, on which were scattered some beautiful old rugs. It was attractively furnished with period pieces.

The diamond-leaded windows were open wide, letting in

the balmy air. They looked over pleasantly rolling parkland, golden as honey in the late-afternoon sun.

But, oblivious to the view, Fran was wondering how long Kirk was likely to be. What should she do for the best?

After a minute or two's thought she decided not to do or say anything until he got here. It was his place to tell their host about the change of plan and complete the business in hand.

In the meantime she would have to go down and explain that he'd been delayed. But first she must tidy herself up.

Opening a communicating door, she discovered a modern, well-appointed bathroom. The thought of a shower and a complete change of clothing was an appealing one, but, afraid of keeping her host waiting, she decided that for the moment she would just repair the obvious damage.

Hastily she washed her face and hands and sponged her knees, wincing as the soap stung her various grazes. Then, having brushed the dust from her dress and jacket, she put on fresh tights and court shoes, tidied her hair, adjusted the wispy scarf and made her way down the stairs.

As she crossed the hall Mortimer appeared, and, opening a handsome pair of double doors, ushered her into the living room. She smiled her thanks, and with a slight inclination of his head he closed them again behind her.

The long, low-ceilinged room, which was at the rear of the house, was cool and dim, and at first glance appeared to be empty. Then a tall, dark-haired man stepped in from the terrace and advanced to meet her.

His back was to the light, his face in shadow.

She had pictured the owner of Balantyne Hall as being on the wrong side of forty, an unprepossessing man, stiff and lacking warmth, whose only assets were wealth and position.

Her first impression of this man was that he was quite young; her second, and even more unexpected, was that he was extremely attractive, with an air of raw power, of breathtaking masculinity.

'Miss Holt? Welcome to Balantyne.' He held out a strong, well-shaped hand.

As his fingers closed around hers she looked up into a lean, devilishly handsome face, with a long, mobile mouth and fascinating thickly lashed eyes.

A face she knew and had thought never to see again.

The shock was a severe one, making her heart start to race and every nerve tighten in rejection. What on earth was Blaze Rawdon doing here?

His dark grey eyes mocking her confusion, he remarked, 'You look surprised to see me.'

Somehow she found her voice. 'I thought you lived in the States.'

'I do—at least for some of the time.'

'I suppose you're here for the party?' She blurted out the first thing that came into her head.

'You could say that.'

Still holding her hand, he looked her over from head to toe. Then, turning her palm uppermost, he examined the graze, remarking sardonically, 'Dear me, you *have* been in the wars.'

'I was about to get into a taxi at the airport when I was pushed over and my bag was snatched,' she explained a shade jerkily. Then instantly wished she'd kept quiet about the little incident.

Level brows drawing together in a frown, he asked, 'Where was Varley when it happened? I understood you were meeting him?'

So he knew about Kirk. Withdrawing her hand as soon as his grip would allow, she said, 'There was a message to say he was delayed.'

'Delayed? Dear me... So you came along to bravely hold the fort?'

Thrown by the open mockery, she stayed silent.

'How long will it be before he gets here?'

'I'm afraid I don't know. But I'm sure he'll get here as soon as he can.'

'It must be nice to feel so confident.' Once again there was that unaccountable derision.

Feeling totally out of her depth, she went back to practicalities. 'The butler said Mr Balantyne was here.'

Eyes glinting, Blaze agreed, 'The butler's right.'

It took a moment or two to sink in. Even then she couldn't believe it. How could Blaze Rawdon, the American businessman, be Edward Balantyne the English aristocrat?

'You don't mean...?' She tried again. 'You can't be...'

He smiled like a tiger. 'I assure you, I can.'

Reeling under this second shock, she said weakly, 'I don't understand.'

'There's some tea on the terrace.' He mimicked an Oxford accent. 'Come and have a cup while I explain.' A hand at her waist, he escorted her outside.

That light but sure touch, and the easy way he dwarfed her five feet seven, made a shiver run down her spine.

Three years apart and a bitter determination to put him right out of her mind had helped her to forget just how tall he was, what a powerful impact he had on her senses.

Now she remembered. Only too well.

Beyond the encircling drive, the ground sloped away, and the paved terrace, with its stone balustrade, overlooked a smooth sweep of green lawns.

Waiting on a table in the shade of an umbrella was a teatray set with a silver teapot and delicate china.

Blaze indicated a comfortable-looking reclining chair, which she sank into gratefully, and asked, 'Milk or lemon?'

'Lemon, please.'

She'd always thought of him as one hundred per cent American, and a city man. But, dressed with casual elegance and quite at home in this very rural setting, apart from a certain toughness he looked every inch the English country gentleman.

Having poured the tea and handed her a cup, with wry self-mockery, he offered her a wafer-thin cucumber sandwich.

When she politely refused he dropped into the seat next to hers, taking one himself and remarking ironically, 'I prefer sandwiches to sweet cakes, proving beyond doubt that I'm English to the core.'

Still trying to gather her scattered wits, she said, 'I thought you were a native New Yorker.'

He shook his head. 'I was born here, at Balantyne Hall, the son of Sir Edward Balantyne. My father was a quiet, austere man who disliked the social whirl; my mother was a beautiful New York butterfly, fun-loving and gregarious. They met at the Waldorf and, proving that opposites attract, fell in love at first sight.'

His mouth twisted. 'Their marriage, which must have been doomed from the start, was hailed by the media as the love-match of the decade. I was born a year later and christened Edward Blaze. Proving, if proof was needed, that a rift already existed, my father always referred to me as Edward while my mother called me Blaze.

'When I was eight my mother took me to the States for a holiday, and we stayed there. My father wanted me back, and a long, bitter battle was fought in the courts. My mother accused him of mental cruelty, and swore that he treated me harshly. With the help of some smart lawyers hired by my maternal grandfather, and a sympathetic judge, my mother won.

'After the divorce she married John Rawdon, who adopted me. This time she chose more carefully, and the marriage was a happy one.

'Two years ago my real father died a lonely, embittered man. He had never married again and had no other children. He left Balantyne Hall and the entire estate to me, expressing a wish that I should revert to using the name Edward Balantyne.

'I felt, in the circumstances, it was the least I could do...'

Derisively, he added, 'And the moral of the story is, never marry for love. It's the most treacherous of all emotions... And speaking of marrying...' Leaning towards her, he picked up her left hand—a slender hand, with long, tapering fingers and polished oval nails—and studied the modest ring. 'Who's the lucky man?'

'Kirk Varley.'

'Really?' Blaze raised a dark brow. 'I would have expected the owner of a jewellery firm to have produced something a little more...shall we say...lavish?'

Fran sprang to her fiancé's defence. 'Kirk only gave it to me just before he left for his business trip. He said I could choose something bigger and better when he got back.'

'And will you?'

She lifted her chin. 'I'm quite happy with this. I don't need anything bigger and better.'

'Most women want a ring they can be proud of.'

Recalling the magnificent ruby that Melinda Ross wore, Fran bit her lip before retorting, 'I'm proud of this. It proves Kirk loves me and—'

'I would have said it proves quite the opposite,' Blaze broke in smoothly. 'In my opinion, if he loved you he would have taken a great deal more care.'

Moving the ring around between his forefinger and thumb, he added contemptuously, 'I've seen better rings come out of Christmas crackers. And it doesn't even fit.'

Her clear grey-green eyes sparkling with fury, she snatched her hand away. 'Do you make a point of being deliberately rude to your guests?'

'Not as a rule.' He sounded unmoved by her anger. 'But in the circumstances I don't think it will be possible to treat you as an ordinary guest.'

Before she could ask him what he meant, he changed the subject to ask, 'So when is my necklace being delivered? When I spoke to Varley he assured me it would be tonight.'

'That's right,' she agreed evenly, though her heart had started to beat faster.

Blaze said flatly, 'The security firm I hired say they know absolutely nothing about it.'

Fran tried to put a bold face on it. 'Wasn't the agreement simply that Varleys were to be responsible for its safe return?'

'Not altogether. The agreement was that Rayburn Security, who delivered it *to* Varleys, would collect it *from* them and return it here. Varleys were to be responsible for the arrangements and the timing. Instead of keeping to that, I find Varley hasn't even contacted the firm. I want to know why not.'

She swallowed hard. 'Kirk made other plans.'

'Without consulting me?'

'He said if there was likely to be a problem he'd clear it with you...'

'Big of him.'

'But he was certain there wouldn't be.'

Blaze's brilliant dark eyes narrowed. 'So what were these other plans?'

Convinced now that he would be furious if he discovered the truth, she played for time. 'I'm sure Kirk will explain everything when he gets here.'

'You seem to have great faith in him. I only hope it's justified.'

Remembering the way her bag had been snatched, she shuddered inwardly, before answering firmly, 'I'm sure it is.'

His expression wry, Blaze said, 'Tell me, Francesca, when did you start working for Varley?'

Only too glad to leave the subject of the necklace, she answered, 'At the beginning of last August.'

'How did you become a jewellery designer?'

'I took a special two-year course at the Welbeck College of Art.'

Frowning, he admitted, 'I would never have associated you with that kind of thing.'

'But you did know *I* was redesigning the necklace. You *must* have known. You weren't at all surprised to see me.'

'Yes, I knew. When Melinda first mentioned your name she also showed me a magazine article about you, entitled, "A Designing Woman". There was a picture...'

He studied her thoughtfully. 'Why the sudden switch? You were a dedicated businesswoman when I knew you.'

'Designing was something I'd always been interested in and had a flair for.'

It was the truth. But not the whole truth. Three years ago, her world in ruins, she had needed a complete and drastic change. A metamorphosis.

She had been twenty-three then, and working in the City for a firm of market analysts. A woman in a man's world, with a job she had competed for and won fair and square against strong male opposition.

Then Blaze had taken over the company to add to his growing empire.

She had been leaving a little late one Friday evening when a malfunctioning lift had trapped them between floors.

As the lift had juddered to a halt he had pressed the alarm button and turned to smile reassuringly at her.

Recognising him immediately, she might have felt tongue-tied and overawed if there hadn't been such an instant rapport.

After identifying her, he had asked about her job, seeking her opinion on company policy and on some of the problems they were facing before moving on to more personal topics.

Normally fairly shy and reticent, something about him had made her sparkle, had made her prettier, wittier than she was.

They had struck sparks off each other.

By the time they'd been released, some three-quarters of an hour later, they had been talking with an ease that had amazed her when she thought about it later.

As soon as the lift had settled jerkily into place and the doors had slid open Blaze had thanked the engineer and, taking Fran's hand, said with smiling authority, 'Now, as you're much too beautiful to starve, I intend to feed you before I take you home.'

His words, and the fact that he'd thought her beautiful, had bowled her over, and she had made no attempt to refuse.

Indeed, she had already been lost. Dazzled. Aware that her life had changed—channelled from the safe and predictable into something a great deal more dangerous and exciting.

Just one look from those grey eyes, so dark yet so brilliant, had destroyed all her previous inaccessibility. Just one touch from those skilled and experienced hands had turned her strongly held beliefs upside down.

His charm, his assurance, had stripped away her defences then, as later they would strip off her clothes.

At first it had been like a fairy tale, full of magic and enchantment and a singing happiness. Loving him had seemed so natural, so right, something she had been born to do.

All her mother's oft-recited woes, the carefully instilled fear and caution, had been forgotten. His passion and his obvious joy in her had made her inhibitions and repressions vanish like morning mist dispersed by the warmth of the sun.

He had made her first time so easy. So wonderful. Lying with him had been like a wanderer coming home, something she had longed for all her life without realising it.

He'd been a caring and tender lover, and his every touch had added to her pleasure until the driving force of his body had brought her an exquisite delight, a rapturous bliss that had excelled her wildest dreams. Then his arms had been her heaven, his shoulder the perfect pillow for her head...

No! No! She mustn't remember. She *never* let herself remember.

Gasping like a swimmer who had been under water too long, she looked up and met grey eyes that had darkened almost to black, as if he too had been reliving the past.

Somehow she dragged her gaze away and looked at her watch. Her voice sounding as if it didn't belong to her, she remarked with as much conviction as she could muster, 'I don't suppose Kirk will be much longer. Whatever delayed him, hopefully he'll be on the next plane.'

'Hopefully.' With a twisted smile, Blaze added, 'But I won't hold my breath.'

Fran was profoundly disturbed by that smile, by the growing certainty that there was something odd going on, something she didn't begin to understand.

On the verge of asking point-blank for an explanation, she chickened out, her nerve failing. Whatever it was, she would wait for Kirk to arrive and let *him* handle it.

CHAPTER TWO

IN THE meantime, however, she had to cope alone. It was a daunting task, made infinitely worse by the trauma of the past.

If she'd had the faintest idea that Blaze Rawdon and Edward Balantyne were one and the same, no power on earth would have induced her to come.

But, as she hadn't, there was nothing to do but make the best of it. That thought in mind, Fran sought for a relatively safe topic of conversation.

'I'd understood *your* fiancée would be here?'

'While I was away Melinda found the country too quiet for her. She's been spending her time between Manchester and London, shopping for her trousseau.

'She was planning to drive from town and get here mid-afternoon. But, as you've probably noticed yourself, she's invariably late.' His little smile was tolerant.

Stretching long legs, he added idly, 'You've met her several times. What did you think of her?'

'She's beautiful.'

'Did you like her?'

Melinda had been open, friendly and vivacious, and, in spite of her apparent lack of principles, Fran had found it impossible to dislike her.

Now she answered honestly, 'Yes, I did.'

'Most people do. As far as men go, that's understandable, but women usually get on well with her. Which surprised me at first, until I realised that though she has her faults she isn't bitchy. Unlike Sherrye...'

Sherrye...

Fran still reacted to that name with a feeling of dread and bitter shame. Though it had been three years ago, that ugly and degrading little scene was still fresh in her mind.

The usual Monday morning meeting had started, but for once her mind hadn't been on the business in hand. Gloriously happy, secure in the knowledge that Blaze loved and wanted her, her thoughts had gone back to the previous night.

'I have to go to Hong Kong Monday evening,' he'd told her regretfully. 'But I'll be back on Friday, and we'll enjoy a quiet few days in the Cotswolds.'

Smiling to herself, Fran was anticipating all the pleasure in store when the double doors of the conference room were flung open and a tall, strikingly beautiful woman with black hair and a vermilion mouth stormed in.

Ignoring the rest of the people grouped round the long table, she singled Fran out and hurled a string of abuse at her, calling her names that made her cheeks burn.

Taken aback by the suddenness of the attack, from a women she had never met and of whose existence she had been completely unaware, Fran sat flushed and mute while the shrill voice ranted on.

'Believe me, I've no intention of letting some two-bit nobody try to steal my fiancé while my back's turned. I know he took you to Paris for the weekend, but don't think for one goddamned minute he's serious about you. He's just been having a fling...

'See this?' She thrust a huge diamond solitaire under Fran's nose. 'Blaze is mine, and now I've joined him he won't want *you* hanging around... Do I make myself clear?'

Turning on her heel, she said over her shoulder, 'If you've got any sense you'll go now, and save him the trouble of having to get rid of you...'

Hips swaying, she walked away, leaving a stunned silence behind her.

'Who the hell was that?' one of the startled analysts asked.

His neighbour, Don Rogers, apparently better informed than the rest, answered, 'Sherrye Kaufmann. Our new boss's fiancée, would you believe? I bumped into them a couple of times when I was in New York earlier this year.'

'She seems to be a first-class bitch.'

'If you knew Rawdon as well as I do, you'd keep opinions like that to yourself,' Don warned.

'Now he's in charge, if you get on the wrong side of either him or Miss Kaufmann you may find your position here becomes intolerable.'

With that reminder, all eyes turned to the remaining protagonist, who was still sitting shocked and dazed.

Becoming aware that she was now the focus of attention, Fran glanced around to find her peers were judging her.

Some were surprised, some curious, one or two—including her own PA—were sympathetic; the remainder were frankly condemning. She had caused her immediate boss and the company as a whole trouble and embarrassment, not only by her actions but by being so publicly humiliated.

Gathering together the reports that lay on the table in front of her, she pushed back her chair and rose to her feet, a slim, businesslike figure in a navy blue suit and white blouse.

Shoulders squared, chin held high, addressing her own departmental head, she said steadily, 'Please accept both my apologies and my resignation.'

She made her way from the room, the imposing double doors clicking to quietly behind her, and, looking neither to right nor left, returned to her office.

Having placed the reports neatly on the desk, she was

gathering up her coat and personal belongings when her PA hurried in.

Over the past couple of years the two women had become friends, and, clearly distressed, Joanna burst out, 'I could kill that two-timing swine—*and* his fiancée...'

Fran, unable to speak, gave the other woman a quick hug.

Crossing the main lobby for the last time, heels clicking on the tiles, she passed Sherrye Kaufmann, whose dark, glittering glance held undisguised triumph.

Then, in a state of shock, feeling no pain *yet*, she walked away from friends and colleagues; from a hard-won job she had enjoyed and been good at; from a man she had trusted and given her heart to.

It seemed her mother had been only too right when she'd preached the doctrine that men were deceivers and women fools to trust them...

'I dare say you remember Sherrye?' Blaze's question broke into her bleak thoughts.

'How could I forget her?' Fran answered wryly, and, knowing he must have had a full account of what had taken place, felt her colour rise.

'Do you still hate her?'

'I never did.' Oddly enough it was the truth.

'You had every right to. Her outrageous behaviour cost you your job.'

'My own stupidity did that,' Fran said crisply.

Dark grey eyes on her half-averted face, he pursued, 'So you didn't blame her?'

Full of shame and guilt, of self-reproach and bitter regret at her own culpability, Fran had set the burden of blame squarely on her own shoulders.

'On the contrary. When I thought about it I felt sorry for her.'

'Sorry for her?' Blaze sounded staggered.

Turning towards him, she said flatly, 'For loving a man who, as soon as his fiancée's back was turned, was more than willing to seduce any woman who came along.'

Despite her attempt to speak dispassionately, her anger and disillusionment at his perfidy came through.

His attractive face hardened. 'Now there you're wrong—on all counts. Firstly, you weren't just *any woman*, as I would have told you at the time had you stopped to listen. Secondly, Sherrye loved my money and the lifestyle I could offer her. Never *me*. Thirdly, our engagement was ended before I left the States. Otherwise she would have travelled with me.'

'Ended?'

'When we first became engaged I warned her that I wouldn't stand for her sleeping around. One afternoon I walked in unexpectedly and caught her in bed with the houseboy. I ordered her to take her things and get out. Though she cried, swore such a thing would never happen again and begged me to change my mind, as far as I was concerned the whole thing was over.'

'She was still wearing your ring.'

'I told her to keep it.' With a twisted smile, he added, 'A kind of payment for services rendered. She didn't think it was enough, and threatened to sue me. I invited her to go ahead. Knowing there was no way she could win, she waited for a while, hoping I'd cool off, before following me to England to try to persuade me to take her back.

'The scene she kicked up in the boardroom was almost certainly caused partly by anger and jealousy at the thought that she'd been replaced, and partly in the hope of driving you away. When she succeeded she must have been cock-a-hoop; she certainly looked it when she arrived at my flat. Finding I was just about to start for the airport, she offered to go to Hong Kong with me.

'I knew she meant trouble, so I told her in no uncertain terms to get out of my life and stay out.

'Unfortunately, though I didn't know it then, the damage was already done...

'It wasn't until I got back from my trip and had a word with your PA that I discovered what had happened. I went straight round to your flat. Your landlord said you'd moved out the previous day and left no forwarding address.

'I tried to find you, but obviously I looked in the wrong places.'

An iron band tightened round Fran's ribs, restricting her breathing. Was it possible he'd *cared*?

In a strangled voice, she asked, 'Why did you try to find me?'

'Why do you think?'

She shook her head mutely.

'Perhaps I didn't like the idea of being misjudged,' he said mockingly. Then, with an abrupt change of subject, 'What do you know about Varley's affairs?'

'Affairs?' She was startled, and showed it.

'I meant *business* affairs.'

'Why n-nothing,' she stammered.

'You don't mean to tell me you weren't aware that the firm's on the verge of bankruptcy?'

'Bankruptcy? I don't believe it! I'm sure it's nothing of the kind.' But, even as Fran strenuously denied the charge, she recalled Kirk saying, 'Trade hasn't been up to much for the past year or so...'

His face stern, Blaze went on relentlessly, 'The business has been going steadily downhill ever since the old man died and his son took over. For one thing, Varley's no businessman, and for another, he's a great deal too fond of the good life.'

Catching a glimpse of Fran's expression, Blaze suggested drily, 'You think that's an instance of the pot calling the kettle black?'

'Isn't it?'

He grinned briefly. 'The difference is, the pot can afford it; the kettle can't. Varley tried gambling to help finance his more expensive tastes—'

'Gambling?' She was horrified.

'It proved to be a big mistake. He began to mix with an unsavoury crowd, people on the fringes of the under-world...'

Fran shook her head, not wanting to believe it. Refusing to believe it.

But Blaze continued regardless, 'He's run up massive debts, both business and private, with damn-all assets.'

'There's the stock.' Even as she spoke she recalled Kirk explaining to the staff that because of the slump in trade he was keeping stock to a minimum.

'A drop in the ocean compared to what he owes,' Blaze said dismissively.

She battled on. 'He has a luxurious apartment.'

'Which is mortgaged up to the hilt.'

Her mouth dry, she demanded, 'How do you know all this?'

'Before I agreed to let Varleys redesign the necklace I hired Ritters Detective Agency to check the firm out. A report came back that the business was an old-established family concern with a reputation for absolute soundness and integrity. It was only later, when I was alerted by a chance remark made by one of my financial advisors, that I instructed the agency to dig deeper.

'Varley had been both clever and careful, and it took them some time to uncover the true state of affairs. Even when they did there was a slip-up, and I didn't get the information until a couple of days ago.'

Struggling to take in what she'd just heard, Fran muttered dazedly, 'I just can't believe it. There *must* be some mistake.'

'There's no mistake.'

She tried not to be shaken by his absolute certainty. 'But even if what you say is true, and I'm quite sure it isn't, what difference can it make? To *you*, I mean...'

'My dear Francesca, I've always given you credit for being an intelligent woman.'

'I don't know what you're getting at.'

He laughed, with a gleam of white healthy teeth. 'I must congratulate you.'

Genuinely bewildered, she echoed, 'Congratulate me? On what?'

'On your acting ability. Did your college curriculum include drama lessons?'

'I really don't know what you mean,' she said stiffly.

'I mean Varley would be proud of you... And, speaking of Varley, don't you think it's odd that he hasn't turned up yet? You've been here for quite a while.'

'Surely it depends on what delayed him?'

'He hasn't even phoned.'

'He may not have had the chance.'

Blaze sketched an ironic salute. 'You're also very loyal, and though I think your loyalty is misplaced, I admire you for it.'

'You're much too kind,' she said drily.

'And you're much too sassy.' His tone held a hint of steel, his words a veiled threat that made her wish she'd kept quiet.

Oh, where on earth was Kirk? she wondered with something close to desperation. If only he'd come...

Rising to his feet, tall and dark and formidable, a force to be reckoned with, Blaze suggested, 'Suppose we take a stroll? Stretch our legs before dinner?' His tone was now pleasantly neutral.

Rather than taking a stroll with him, she would have preferred to escape from his disturbing presence and be alone.

So much had happened that she felt almost giddy with the strain of trying to keep abreast of things. She longed for time to evaluate and hopefully disprove Blaze's allegations that Kirk was on the verge of bankruptcy, to dismiss all this ridiculous talk of gambling and the underworld...

She wanted a chance to think, to put into perspective what she'd learnt about his engagement to Sherrye, to reflect on how different her own future might have been had she stood her ground instead of running...

But, perhaps most of all, she needed to try and make sense of her host's enigmatic behaviour, and the strange undercurrents she could sense...

Becoming aware that he was watching her face and waiting, and knowing she could hardly tell him the truth, she hurriedly sought for a convincing reason not to go.

'I think I'd sooner rest quietly in my room. When my bag was snatched I scraped my knees, and they're starting to feel stiff...'

Blaze's wry expression suggested he knew an excuse when he heard one.

'Let me see.' He went down on his haunches by her chair, and before she could object brushed aside her skirt. 'Dear, dear...' Studying the grazes on her smooth, shapely knees, he tutted.

Then, head tilted back, he glanced up at her and, his eyes gleaming between thick, dark lashes, announced with mock gravity, 'However, I don't think your injuries are serious enough to prevent you taking a walk.'

Straightening up, too close for comfort, he offered her a hand, adding, 'In fact a bit of exercise might loosen things up, do you a world of good.'

Biting her lip in vexation, but seeing nothing for it, she

took the proffered hand and tried not to shiver at the tingle his touch caused as he pulled her to her feet.

Reluctantly, and in silence, she was following him across the terrace when a young maid appeared to clear away the tea things.

Blaze paused. 'Oh, Hannah,' he said pleasantly, 'will you ask Cook to hold dinner until I give the word?'

The girl made a little bob.

Turning to Fran, his smile quizzical, he added, 'Must allow the missing pair every chance to get here, don't you think?'

His hand at her waist, he escorted her down a shallow flight of stone steps and across the driveway. A moment later they were walking on smoothly shaven green lawns.

The sun was low on the horizon, its oblique rays making the trees cast long, dark shadows, but the early evening air was still golden and balmy. A warm breeze played with the ends of Fran's scarf and ruffled Blaze's dark hair, making him look even more attractive.

'Shall we head for the lake?' he asked.

'Whatever you say.'

Grey eyes amused, he murmured, 'I do like a tractable woman.'

Fran spoke without thinking. 'Nice as she is, from what I've seen of her, I wouldn't put Miss Ross in that category.'

'And you would be quite right,' he agreed smoothly. 'Melinda has a will of her own and a very clear idea of what she wants.'

'And you don't find that a handicap?'

Smiling a little at the irony, he answered cheerfully, 'On the contrary. A wife who is too compliant would be a bore. I wanted a woman who was compatible, and basically good-tempered, but with enough spice to make life interesting.'

'It sounds as though you chose with your head rather than your heart,' she observed.

'Anyone who doesn't is a fool.'

'Then you've never been in love?'

His expression sardonic, he said, 'Oh, yes, I have. But I don't believe that love necessarily makes for a happy marriage...'

Remembering what he'd told her about his parents' marriage, she wasn't surprised.

'Or lack of love, an unhappy one,' he added with an air of finality.

She chose her words with care. 'So you would be happy to marry without love if all the other factors were present?'

'It makes more sense than marrying for love when they're not.'

'You wouldn't wait and hope to find both?'

'That would be the ideal, of course, but it happens so rarely.' His face grew sombre. 'And then it doesn't always work out. In my considered opinion, love is best left out of the equation.'

'Suppose your chosen partner didn't feel the same?'

'One-sided loving, you mean? To be steered clear of at all costs! It unbalances a relationship and can only cause trouble when one partner wants more than the other can give. If both partners go into marriage with a set of clearly defined rules and no emotional hang-ups,' he went on briskly, 'it's much more likely to succeed.'

His words only confirmed what Melinda had already made plain: that their forthcoming marriage was in the nature of a carefully planned merger.

With a little shiver, Fran objected, 'It sounds too much like some kind of business deal.'

'And why not? Why shouldn't I plan my marriage with as much care as I plan my business deals? As I make many deals, and I only intend to get married once, it's a great deal more important.'

How could a man she knew was quite capable of being warm and romantic act this way? 'It just seems so…so cold and unfeeling.'

'Oh, I don't think it will be that.' His sideways glance was mocking. 'There's enough passion on both sides to guarantee good sex. What more could anyone ask?'

In Fran's opinion, a great deal. She had always believed that love and sex went hand in hand, that sex alone was unfulfilling, as disappointing as an empty fire-grate on a snowy day.

'Just suppose, when it was too late, one of you fell in love with someone else?'

'That would be a complication,' Blaze admitted. 'But hopefully we wouldn't let it make any difference. No matter what the poets would have us believe, it should be possible to stifle unwanted feelings… You look doubtful?'

'No, I'm sure you're right.' It wasn't easy, in fact it was the hardest thing she'd ever done, but it *was* possible.

He raised a dark brow. 'Do I detect a shift in attitude? Have I converted you to my way of thinking?'

Shaking her head, she said, 'I still don't believe you can deal with human emotions as though they were figures on a balance sheet. At least not long-term. And, to me, marriage should be a commitment that lasts a lifetime.'

'Well, there at least we see eye to eye.'

Something more fundamental than mere curiosity drove her to ask, 'Then you don't visualise an open marriage?'

'You mean with both partners free to roam?'

She nodded.

'No, I don't,' he said shortly. 'I'm prepared to stick as closely as possible to the vows I've made, and I expect my wife to do the same. As well as fun and excitement, I want a stable marriage and a happy home for our children.'

Recalling the day she and Kirk had been lunching with Melinda, and a small child had been sitting with her parents at the next table, Fran's heart sank.

The little girl, chubby and dimpled, had turned a big, beaming smile in their direction. Fran had smiled back, but Melinda had merely looked uncomfortable.

'Not fond of children?' Kirk had asked.

'No, I'm not,' the American had admitted with disarming frankness. 'But as I need this marriage to go through, I didn't think it would be wise to say so. An agreement to have children is written into the settlement the lawyers drew up.' She had pulled a face.

'Of course, I can stall for as long as possible, but my future husband is far from being a fool. Sooner or later he's going to realise that I've no intention of sticking to the bargain, and then there'll be heap-big trouble.

'Though he can be extremely generous—he bought me the Porsche for a wedding present—he can also be quite formidable when he's crossed. If things get too hot I may have to cut and run...'

Fran had felt disturbed and off-put. From whichever angle she'd looked at it, that kind of cold and calculated 'bargain' had seemed somehow distasteful.

Finding herself unable to condone the other woman's lack of principle, and feeling precious little sympathy for Edward Balantyne, she had made an effort to put what was really no business of hers out of her mind.

Now she felt a sudden sharp concern.

It just went to prove that a business-type settlement could fall down where a loving talk might have brought things into the open...

Becoming aware that Blaze seemed to be waiting for an answer to a question she hadn't even heard, Fran said vaguely, 'I'm sorry?'

'I asked, was your parents' marriage a good one? Did

you have a happy home? It's something you've never talked about.'

'No, it wasn't happy,' she admitted. 'My mother was a single parent. When her lover discovered she was pregnant, instead of standing by her he left her flat. He didn't even help financially.

'Being abandoned to bring up a child alone made her warped and bitter. Afraid that I would make the same mistake, she drummed it into me that men weren't to be trusted...'

'I see,' Blaze said slowly.

Flushing a little as she recalled their first meeting and her own unrestrained response to his lovemaking, she added a shade awkwardly, 'You may not believe that.'

'Oh, but I do. And it explains something that's always puzzled me... Why such a passionate woman was still a virgin at twenty-three.'

As her colour deepened still further he harked back to ask, 'So what plans have you for your marriage?'

'None as yet. Everything's happened so quickly... Though Kirk suggested a spring wedding.'

'Are you living together?'

The blunt question threw her somewhat, but, recalling *his* frankness, she found herself answering, 'No... Yes... Well, we will be.'

Blaze lifted a quizzical brow.

'Kirk asked me to move in with him, and he helped me take my things over to his place just before he left for the airport.'

'But you're not yet living at his apartment.' It was a statement rather than a question.

'Well, no. I didn't want to actually move in until he came back, so I stayed in my own flat last night and only handed in the keys this morning.'

'And now you're looking forward to him getting back,

so that after this weekend's out of the way you can be together?'

Suspecting hidden mockery, she nevertheless answered as steadily as possible, 'Yes, I am.'

They had reached the man-made lake, an elongated figure of eight, the narrowest part spanned by a mellow stone bridge with three arches.

Its looking glass surface was marred by an occasional ripple as the light breeze skittered over it. Patches of late water lilies, their dark green pads and perfect waxy blooms looking almost artificial, formed floating islands.

The expanse of blue water was surrounded by a paved walkway with herbaceous borders, stone benches and old statuary. Beyond the low walls were ornamental trees and beautifully terraced gardens.

'It's always referred to as "the lake",' Blaze remarked, as they began to follow the path round it, 'though really it's little more than a pond.'

Reaching a honeysuckle-entwined arbour, he sat down, and, indicating the space beside him suggested straight-faced, 'It might be as well to rest those knees a little.'

Knowing she'd invited his derision, Fran hid her chagrin and joined him on the sun-warmed marble bench, keeping a careful distance between them.

For a while they sat without speaking, watching brilliant blue dragonflies darting over the water, whirring like tiny helicopters. Then Blaze broke the lengthening silence to ask, 'So how do you see your relationship with Varley?'

She hesitated. 'I'm not sure what you mean.'

'Do you see it as a wildly romantic love affair, or as something more...shall we say...mundane?'

'I'm in love with Kirk, if that's what you're getting at,' she answered stiffly. 'I wouldn't be marrying him otherwise.'

'And how does *he* feel? Is he in love with you?'

About to say *Of course*, she paused. He'd never actually said so... But he *must* love her, otherwise why had he asked her to marry him?

Cocking a dark brow, Blaze commented, 'You seem a bit doubtful?'

'Not at all,' she denied hurriedly. 'I'm quite sure he loves me.'

'Do you intend to have children?' Blaze probed.

'I hope so, eventually.'

'How does Varley feel about children?'

'I'm not quite sure,' she admitted.

'You don't seem to know him very well.'

'We haven't really had a chance to discuss it.'

'How long have you been going out together?'

'Not long,' she replied, purposely vague.

'Five months? Six months?'

'A few weeks.'

Blaze picked it up, as she'd known he would. 'But didn't you say you'd been working for him since last August?'

'Yes.'

'What took him so long?'

Aware of his piercing stare, she shrugged, and trying for nonchalance, spoke the exact truth. 'I was just another employee. I don't think Kirk had ever really noticed me until I started to work on the designs for the necklace.'

'I *see*. But you'd noticed him?'

Flushing a little, she said nothing.

'Tell me, Francesca, how old is Varley?'

'He was thirty-two at the beginning of September. The same as you.'

Blaze quirked a brow and she bit her lip, wishing she hadn't revealed the fact that she'd remembered his birthday.

'What's he like?'

'Intelligent, witty, sociable, fun to be with, a man who makes a lot of friends—'

'Mostly women-friends…' Blaze watched her generous mouth tighten, before adding, 'Or so the detective agency told me.'

'I've no doubt the detective agency was wrong about a lot of things—'

'It's possible, but not probable.'

Ignoring the interruption, she went on angrily, 'And, whatever they told you, Kirk's no womaniser. He's caring and responsible, he *respects* women…'

'I see! As you're planning to be married, I wondered why you hadn't yet been to bed together.'

Infuriated by his open mockery, she pointed out, 'You asked me whether we were *living* together, not *sleeping* together.'

'So I did… And are you?'

'Of course. Don't most engaged couples these days?' Blaze's expression didn't change, but she was oddly convinced that the thought of her sleeping with the other man had made him furious.

Just for an instant she wanted to admit that it was a lie. But if she did he would only go back to making fun of Kirk.

A tendril of curly ash-brown hair had escaped from the restraining knot, and the breeze blew it across her hot cheek. Before she could brush it away Blaze took the errant strand between his finger and thumb, and while she sat frozen, unnaturally still, began to toy with it.

With sudden painful clarity she recalled how in the past, when *they* had made love, he'd always liked to play with her thick sun-streaked hair, saying it felt like spun silk.

Apparently content with the response he had evoked, he tucked the strand behind her ear, before enquiring coolly, 'Leaving Varley's character aside, what's he like to look at?'

The tension snapped like an overstretched rubber band. 'Surely your detective told you?' she demanded waspishly.

Unruffled, he said, 'I'd like to hear your version.'

'Kirk's your exact opposite…' Was that why she'd chosen him? Pushing the treacherous thought away, she went on determinedly, 'He's not too tall, slimly built, with blond hair, light blue eyes, a fair complexion—'

'And oodles of charm, I expect?'

'Oodles,' she agreed evenly, determined not to let her companion's snide comment bother her.

'Melinda found him charming,' Blaze admitted. 'She remarked that he was like a young Robert Redford.'

'Jealous?' Fran enquired sweetly.

'What do you think?'

Of course he wasn't jealous. With his looks and charisma Blaze had no call to be jealous of any man.

'I think most men would be.'

'But then I'm not "most men", and I've learnt how to keep what's mine while I still want it.'

She didn't doubt it.

'What about you, Francesca? Aren't you jealous?'

'You mean of Melinda?'

'I wasn't thinking of Melinda. I meant of all the other women in Varley's life.'

'So far as *I'm* aware, there are no other women.'

'And you still intend to go ahead and marry him?'

'Yes, I do.'

'Then what I told you earlier hasn't made any difference?'

Just for an instant she thought Blaze was referring to what she'd learnt about Sherrye and his previous engagement, and her heart seemed to stop.

Pulling herself together, she stammered, 'A-are you talking about Kirk's financial situation?'

'What else?' Blaze asked laconically.

'No, it hasn't made any difference.'

'You'll be prepared to stand by him when he becomes bankrupt?'

'*If* he becomes bankrupt, I'll certainly be prepared to stand by him.'

'But you still don't believe it?'

'No, I don't believe it!' she stated boldly. 'When Kirk gets here—'

'*If* he gets here.' Blaze used the same emphasis on the same word.

'Of course he'll get here.' The statement, meant to reassure herself as much as Blaze, seemed to echo hollowly. Jumping to her feet, she insisted, 'He's probably here now. And surely Miss Ross will be?'

With no sign of haste, Blaze rose. 'Then perhaps we should start to stroll back. The prettiest way, and as it happens the shortest, is across the bridge and through the rose garden.'

Halfway across the bridge, by tacit consent, they paused to look at the spectacular sunset. Leaning her arms on the stone balustrade, Fran stood entranced.

The sun was slipping towards the horizon, turning the sky into a riot of pink and lavender, interlaced with palest green and wisps of grey chiffon cloud.

As she stared, Blaze moved to stand behind her, his hands on the balustrade either side of her elbows, effectively imprisoning her there.

She straightened, every nerve in her body tightening at his nearness.

He bent closer, and, his cheek brushing hers, asked softly, 'Do you remember that evening in Paris? The sunset?'

She had dammed up the past with misery and pain, with self-reproach and bitter determination, never allowing herself remember. Now, as though his words had breached the dam, she was unable to stop the memory flooding back.

It had been his birthday, and the most wonderful evening of her life. Stretched on a lounger on their private balcony, still glowing from his lovemaking, she had watched the glorious pageant from the luxury of his arms.

Later, her fingers entwined in his, he had shown her the Left Bank by night, before taking her for a trip along the Seine and a romantic candlelit dinner on one of the *bateaux mouches*.

Afterwards they had returned to his small house close to the Île de la Cité and made love again...

Unable to bear the recollection, she turned blindly to escape, only to find herself imprisoned by his arms.

Looking down into her face, he said with soft satisfaction, 'I see you do.'

As she stood helpless, vulnerable, he bent his dark head and, making no attempt to hold her in any way, covered her mouth with his.

CHAPTER THREE

HIS kiss was light, almost casual, with no hint of force or compulsion, yet there was an arrogance about it that claimed her body and soul, and declared complete ownership.

When he drew back she staggered a little, dazed and confused. It took her what seemed an age before she was able to pull herself together and regain some semblance of assurance.

As soon as she could speak, she demanded huskily, 'Why did you do that?'

'An impulse... For old times' sake... Whichever you prefer.'

For whichever reason, she could only wish he'd never done it. It had thrown her completely. Destroyed any remaining certainty or peace of mind.

But she mustn't let past feelings, a passion long over and done with, ruin the present. She must hold on to the here and now, to what she *had* rather than what she might have wanted three years ago.

'I'd prefer it if you would forget the past and resist any further impulses,' she informed him sternly. 'Particularly as I'm engaged, and you're going to be married in a few days' time.'

Brushing aside his arm, she turned to walk away, adding over her shoulder, 'Now I'd like to get back. Kirk's sure to be waiting.'

Falling into step beside her, Blaze taunted, 'I wouldn't bet on it.'

'Well, I would,' she retorted defiantly.

'Then we'll have a small wager. Do you remember the keyring you bought me in Paris? The one with the picture of the Eiffel Tower?'

'Yes, I remember it,' she said huskily. It had been just a cheap souvenir, laughingly bought on the spur of the moment when he'd mentioned it was his birthday.

'Well, if Varley's there I'll give it back to you...'

Her heart lurched painfully. Was it possible that Blaze had kept it all this time?

'If he's not—'

Shaking her head, she objected, 'I can't bet. I have nothing to give you if I lose.'

'Tell you what,' he said lightly, 'if you lose you can give me a kiss.'

Panic-stricken, she began, 'No! I don't—'

'I thought you were certain he *would* be there?' Blaze broke in mockingly.

'I am.'

'So why are you so scared?'

'I'm not scared, but—'

The trap snapped shut. 'Then the wager's on!'

Apparently confident of winning, he made no attempt to hide his triumph.

Realising belatedly that she had been led into this like a lamb to the slaughter, Fran bit her lip.

But why? What was his motive?

He was well aware of the effect his last kiss had had, so it was probably to disconcert her. But why should he want to?

Or could it be that he was simply baiting her? Having some fun at her expense? Waiting to see what her reaction would be if she lost?

Though of course she wouldn't lose, she told herself stoutly as they went through a stone archway and into the walled rose garden.

'I'm afraid it's past its best,' Blaze remarked.

'It's lovely.' Fran let the pleasant scene wash over her, too busy with her thoughts to give it more than a passing accolade.

This weekend was of the utmost importance to Kirk, and he would move heaven and earth not to be later than was absolutely necessary.

He would be waiting, she was sure of it, and able to answer all Blaze's ridiculous suspicions and unfounded allegations. Everything would miraculously right itself, and this uncomfortable day would be unimportant, relegated to the past.

But even as she made an effort to reassure herself Fran knew that no matter what answers Kirk had nothing would ever be quite the same again. At the back of her mind there would always be a lingering regret for what she'd lost, for what might have been...

At the far end of the rose garden a door in the wall gave on to the kitchen garden, with its carefully laid out vegetable plots and fruit bushes.

Beyond the greenhouses was a kind of small covered courtyard at the side of the house, and from there a metal-studded door led into what Fran judged to be the servants' hall.

Several heavy oak dressers were ranged against the walls, a refectory table stood on the stone-flagged floor and the huge fire-grate was filled with logs and pine cones.

They were scarcely inside before Mortimer advanced to meet them purposefully.

'I take it Miss Ross is here?' Blaze asked.

'No, sir. However, there is a gentleman waiting in your study.'

Her heart leaping, Fran gave her companion a swift glance of triumph.

Lifting a dark brow, Blaze enquired satirically, 'A blond, blue-eyed Adonis with oodles of charm?'

'No, sir,' the butler replied, his face impassive, 'A military-looking gentleman. He gave his name as Bellamy and said he'd spoken to you earlier, and you'd asked him to call.'

Blaze nodded his satisfaction. 'Then Mr Varley hasn't arrived?'

'No, sir.'

'Any messages?'

'No, sir, none.'

As Fran's heart sank like a stone, Blaze said, 'Thank you, Mortimer. Will you tell Cook we'll have dinner at eight-thirty?'

The butler bowed his head and retreated soundlessly.

Blaze led Fran through to the main hall and opened the door into the living room. An edge of steel to his voice, he told her, 'I'd like to talk to you. It won't take me long to deal with Bellamy, if you'd care to wait in here.'

Though politely phrased, it was undoubtedly an order.

Her soft mouth firming, she objected, 'I was hoping to have a shower and get changed before dinner.'

'There'll be plenty of time for that after we've talked.'

'Very well,' she said tightly.

Simple and spacious, the living room was a harmonious blend of old and new. It had linenfold panelling, a beamed ceiling and deep window recesses; the doors on to the terrace, which still stood open, though designed with some care, had obviously been added at a much later date.

The carpet was old and venerable, and the delicate antique furniture bore the patina of age, but a modern, comfortable-looking suite stood in front of the huge stone fireplace, and the television and stereo units were state-of-the-art.

Sinking into a low chair, gazing blindly at the huge pottery jug of mixed flowers that filled the hearth, Fran wondered what could possibly have happened to delay Kirk for this length of time.

It seemed so peculiar that he hadn't at least phoned to explain his absence and make his excuses.

Suppose he'd had an accident?

No, she mustn't start thinking like that...

Agitated, too restless to sit still, she jumped to her feet and went out on to the terrace.

The little breeze had died, and the air was warm and still. Already the brightness of the day was being eclipsed, shrouded in blue-grey diaphanous veils.

As she stood watching the September dusk creep stealthily out of hiding, a black London taxi, headlights on and moving slowly, swung round the corner of the house.

Melinda Ross had her own car, so it must be Kirk!

In her eagerness, hurrying down the steps to meet him, Fran missed her footing and landed awkwardly, turning her ankle. Ignoring the stab of pain, she struggled down the remaining steps.

As she reached the bottom, the taxi, which was picking up speed, drew level, and she realised two things simultaneously. Rather than just arriving, it was in fact just leaving, and the occupant definitely wasn't Kirk, but a much older man with smooth silver hair and a neat moustache.

No doubt it was Mr Bellamy departing.

Staring after the vehicle, watching its red rear-lights disappear down the back drive, she frowned. Though she'd glimpsed the passenger's face only fleetingly, it had been strangely familiar.

It took her a little while to place it. When she did she felt a shock of surprise. Blaze's visitor had been her 'colonel', the military-looking man who had helped her to her feet and picked up her case.

Sheer coincidence?

Surely not.

Of course coincidences *did* happen, as much in real life as in fiction, but it was stretching credibility too far to believe that this was one.

But what else could it be?

Fran was still puzzling over it when lights flashed on behind her, and she turned to find Blaze standing in the doorway.

Her ankle distinctly painful now, and threatening to let her down, she went back up the steps with some care.

'Knees still troubling you?' he queried with mock sympathy as he stood aside to let her enter.

'No,' she said shortly. Then, unwilling to sound rude, added, 'I jarred my ankle when I slipped off one of the steps.'

He indicated an armchair. 'Then you'd better sit down.'

She obeyed thankfully.

Taking a seat opposite, he queried, 'How did you come to do that?'

'I saw the taxi and I—' She stopped speaking abruptly.

'Thought it was Varley?' he finished for her.

'Yes,' she admitted.

'Are you really expecting him to come?'

'Of course I'm expecting him to come.'

'Either *you're* a fool or you believe *I* am.'

'I don't know what you're talking about.'

'Look,' he said, a shade impatiently, 'isn't it time to forget this charade and tell me the truth?'

Reaching the end of her tether, she retorted sharply, 'If I knew what charade you were talking about, I might well. I'm fed up with all this...this...mystery...this double-talk. I wish you'd come straight out and say what you mean. What makes you think Kirk *won't* keep to the arrangements?'

Blaze sighed. 'Very well, as you pretend not to know,

I'll lay it on the line. Varley is on the verge of bankruptcy. It would take a miracle to save him—'

'So *you* say.'

Ignoring the interruption, he went on calmly, 'Your fiancé has in his possession a necklace that, with eighteen perfectly matched rubies, is worth a king's ransom. Even sold individually, the stones would raise enough to provide a fresh start in—' he shrugged '—say South America, and, with care, keep him in relative comfort for the rest of his life.'

'You must be joking!' she burst out.

Blaze shook his head. 'In his position anyone might be tempted.'

'You surely don't...' She tried again. 'You *can't* be serious!'

'I'm quite serious.'

'Oh, this is *absurd*! You can't really think that Kirk might be on his way to Buenos Aires or somewhere with the Balantyne rubies in his pocket?'

'That's exactly what I think. I also strongly suspect that he sent *you* here as a cover, to stall for as long as possible.'

'And I suppose you imagine that when the hue and cry has died down I'll be sneaking off to join him?'

'Why not? You're in it together, aren't you?'

Fran laughed incredulously. 'I think you must have been reading too many cheap novels...'

Seeing his face darken with anger, she insisted, 'Honestly, your suspicions are so far off the mark as to be ludicrous.'

For the first time he looked uncertain. 'I could almost believe you mean that.'

'I *do* mean it.'

'Then suppose you give me some straight answers to some straight questions. Why didn't Varley use Rayburn Security, as arranged?'

Knowing quite well what it would sound like, she found herself flushing as she answered. 'He said something about special security costing a great deal of money.'

'How was that a problem when I was paying?'

'P-perhaps he didn't know you were paying.'

'He knew full well that I was meeting all the security costs. It was part of the agreement.'

Seeing she was disconcerted, Blaze pressed home his advantage. 'So, if no security firm was to be involved, what was the plan?'

She moistened dry lips. 'That as we were coming to Balantyne Hall...'

When she hesitated, he urged, 'Do go on.' His voice was smooth as polished glass.

'We should bring it ourselves.'

Watching her like a cat watching a mouse, he said softly, 'I see. It's pretty much what I suspected from the start.'

'In a way it made sense.' She tried to justify the decision. 'As Kirk said, everything had been done with such secrecy that apart from the craftsman who actually reset the stones—'

'That was William Bailey, I understand?' Blaze broke in.

'Yes...and Mr Bailey's been with Varleys for more than forty years. Apart from him, there wasn't another soul who knew anything about the necklace, so Kirk thought it would be safe enough.'

'What did *you* think?'

'I—I wasn't too happy with the plan, but I decided he was probably right. I mean from the point of view of secrecy...'

'So you went along with it.'

'Yes.'

'And now it's gone wrong, and you're left holding the baby, so to speak.'

'It hasn't gone wrong.'

Grimly, Blaze agreed. 'I suppose from *your* point of view it hasn't. However, I don't care for the idea of being robbed, especially of a family heirloom.'

'You haven't been robbed. When Kirk gets here—'

His exasperation evident, Blaze broke in icily, 'Even if you're as innocent as you're trying to make out, it must be obvious by now that's he's *not* going to come. He has the necklace and—'

'But he *hasn't*…!'

Blaze stared at her, taken aback.

'Kirk wasn't carrying the necklace.'

'You mean *you* were?'

'Yes,' she admitted.

'Why?'

'Because he had this business trip he couldn't get out of.'

Reluctant admiration in his voice, Blaze admitted, 'Varley's been a damn sight cleverer than I gave him credit for.'

Uncertain just how to take that remark, Fran said defensively, 'He went to a lot of trouble to make sure the necklace was safe.'

'I bet he did.' His eyes cold and hard as granite, Blaze suggested, 'Perhaps you'll tell me *exactly* what arrangements were made?'

'Before Kirk left for Amsterdam, he packed the necklace up himself and put it in the safe. Then, the following day, just before my taxi arrived to take me to the airport, Mr Bailey opened the safe and gave me the package. Kirk had checked up and found that my plane was due to land about twenty minutes before his, so he asked me to wait for him by the main reception desk—'

'And you were waiting there when you got the message to say he'd been delayed and you were to go on?'

'Yes.'

'What did you do then?'

'I went to get a taxi.'

'And that's when your bag was snatched?'

'Yes.'

He laughed harshly. 'My dear Francesca, do you really expect me to believe that cock and bull story?'

'It happens to be the truth.'

'Oh, yes, I know your bag was snatched, but wasn't the whole thing just a put-up job to account for the necklace being missing? So that the most anyone could accuse either of you of was negligence?'

'No, it wasn't—'

'Oh, come on! You know as well as I do that you never had the necklace in the first place. You were covering up for Varley.'

'That's where you're wrong—'

'But I'm afraid, my sweet, that you made two big mistakes. In the first place you took the whole thing far too calmly. You didn't even report the theft, did you?'

'No.'

'Why not?'

'I didn't want to be held up for ages. You see, I—'

'It would have been a damn sight more convincing if you'd had hysterics and called Airport Security, as anyone who was supposed to have had a priceless necklace stolen would have done.

'In the second place you said nothing to me. When I asked you about the necklace you tried to pretend that everything would be fine when Varley got here. If you'd really had it stolen—'

'But I *hadn't*,' she cried. 'I said I was *carrying* the necklace, but I never said it had been stolen. If you'd only stop and *listen* to me...'

His grey eyes narrowed on her face. 'Okay, I'm listening,' he said curtly. 'And believe me it had better be good.'

'Though Kirk had assured me there was no risk, I was terribly nervous about carrying something so precious in a handbag. I kept wondering if there wasn't a safer way... By the time I got to the airport, I'd made up my mind. I went into the Ladies', took it out of its case and put it on under my dress, which luckily buttons up to the neck. The scarf was useful for hiding any telltale outline...'

'Well, I'll be damned!' he said admiringly. Then, sharply, 'So where is it now? What did you do with it?'

'I wasn't sure what to do with it,' she admitted. 'I didn't want to just leave it lying around in my room, so I decided to let it stay where it was until Kirk got here.'

'You mean you're still wearing it?'

'Yes. I—I hope you don't mind.'

She took off the wisp of scarf, undid the top two buttons of her dress, and reached to unfasten the necklace.

As she fumbled with the safety catch, he said, 'Let me... No, don't get up...'

Suddenly he was standing over her, much too close for comfort. As he released the catch his fingers brushed the warmth of her nape, making her shiver.

Lifting the glittering necklace free, he held it between his long, well-shaped hands while he studied the new design.

The setting was light, almost delicate, but Fran had grouped the rubies in threes, giving them maximum impact and making them look like exotic flowers.

'I hope you like it?' she queried nervously, while, her own hands not quite steady, she refastened her buttons.

'It's absolutely exquisite,' Blaze said slowly. 'You have real talent.'

'Thank you.' She was absurdly pleased by his praise.

Turning those brilliant eyes on her, he demanded, 'Tell me something. Why didn't you give it to me sooner?'

She stated the obvious. 'As owner of the firm, I thought Kirk should be the one to hand it over and complete the business.'

'And wasn't there another reason?'

'Another reason?'

'Weren't you...disinclined, shall we say, to let on that you'd been carrying it?'

It wasn't safe to think while he was in the same room. 'Yes,' she admitted reluctantly. 'Having had my bag snatched...'

'Yes, it wasn't much of a recommendation for Varley's plan. I take it the snatch *was* genuine?'

'Yes, it was,' she said shortly. And could only be grateful for the impulse that had made her decide *not* to carry the necklace in her bag, as Kirk had suggested.

'You didn't seem to be *too* upset, which rather made me wonder.'

A trifle tartly, she told him, 'Having my purse, credit cards, chequebook and driving licence stolen wasn't my idea of fun, but their loss faded into insignificance compared to the necklace...'

'Speaking of which, I'd better put this little bauble away.'

'I'm sorry I don't have the box.'

'A minor problem.' Blaze crossed to the fireplace and touched a hidden button, and to the right of the mantelpiece a section of panelling slid aside to reveal a small safe set in the wall.

Taking out a soft grey leather pouch, he dropped the necklace into it. A moment later the safe door was closed and the panelling in place.

As he turned back to her the grandfather clock in the hall began to strike eight. Blaze frowned. 'If the other two don't get here soon, it looks as though we'll be having dinner *à deux*.'

Shuddering at the thought, she prayed silently, and with great fervour, that the missing pair would turn up without further delay.

The prospect of a meal and maybe an evening alone with Blaze was daunting, to say the least. He wasn't a comfortable companion—she was far too *aware* of him, and the memory of all that lay between them was a traumatic one. For *her* at any rate...

'You mentioned wanting to shower and change.' Blaze's voice broke into her thoughts.

'Yes. Yes, I do,' she said, rising to her feet with more than usual care.

He never missed a thing. 'How is your ankle? Can you make it up to your room? Or would you like me to carry you?'

Just the thought of lying in his arms made her go hot all over. 'No!' Then, more moderately, 'No, thank you, I'll be fine.'

'If you're sure?'

'I'm sure.'

'In that case I'll leave you to it. Will twenty minutes be long enough?'

At her nod, he suggested, 'Then perhaps you'll join me for a pre-dinner drink on the terrace...? In this kind of weather I prefer to be outdoors whenever possible.'

As he moved to touch the bell she turned to escape, afraid he'd change his mind and insist on carrying her.

Ignoring the stabs of pain, she hobbled across the hall and began to climb the stairs, favouring her injured ankle as much as possible.

To add to her troubles her right side was starting to stiffen up, and the inevitable bruises were making themselves felt. By the time she reached her room she was bathed in a cold dew of perspiration.

Standing stork-like whenever practicable, she took off her clothes and showered, ruefully noting the dark bruising on her right hip and arm.

Dried and scented, Fran donned fresh undies and a simple cocktail dress with shoestring straps. She would have preferred to hide the bruises on her arm, but both the evening dresses she'd brought were sleeveless.

She never wore bright lipstick, just a touch of pale lipgloss, and with a flawless complexion, and brows and lashes several shades darker than her hair, as a rule she needed little or no other make-up.

But now, standing in front of the mirror, she made up with care, partly to disguise her paleness and partly to boost her morale, before starting to take her hair into its usual neat coil.

While her hands mechanically performed the routine tasks, she wondered for the umpteenth time where on earth Kirk could be.

Once again the thought returned to haunt her that he might have had an accident of some kind. It would explain why there had been no message...

No! She mustn't start imagining the worst.

But if he was all right why hadn't he at least called to make sure she had got the necklace there safely, and explain his own absence?

It was strange and disturbing.

And there was another thing that was equally strange and disturbing. If Kirk had known full well that Blaze was meeting all the security costs, why hadn't he used Rayburns rather than take the slightest risk?

If she'd left the necklace in her handbag...

But thank the Lord she hadn't.

It was a great relief to have finally handed it over and

know it was no longer her responsibility. And at least by producing it she'd managed to allay some of Blaze's wilder suspicions.

Realising her twenty minutes were almost up, she hurriedly finished pinning her hair and, praying that at least *one* of the missing two had turned up, set off down the stairs.

Grimacing at each step, she battled on, using the polished banister to take as much of her weight as possible.

So intent was she that she had almost reached the hall before she realised that Blaze was standing at the foot of the stairs watching her.

He was wearing a well-cut dinner jacket, a white evening shirt and a black bow tie; he looked handsome, charismatic, and distinctly vexed.

Grimly, he observed, 'I see you'd rather suffer than ask for help.'

'Thank you, but I don't need any help.' She was better at standing on her dignity than her feet.

He gave her a look of exasperation, 'Well, at least take my arm.'

Reluctantly she obeyed, and found herself glad of its support until she was able to hobble on to the terrace and sink into one of the reclining chairs.

Overhead the sky was a clear blue grazed with purple, the sprinkling of stars looking close enough to touch.

Anxiety making Fran blind to the beauty of the evening, she voiced the question uppermost in her mind. 'Have either of the others arrived?'

Hearing the forlorn hope, he said sardonically, 'No, I'm afraid you're stuck with me. However, I'll do my best to make sure you're not bored.'

To Fran's anxious ears the words sounded more like a threat than a promise.

Playing the role of polite host, he crossed to the drinks trolley and asked, 'Now, what will you have?'

Playing the role of polite guest, she answered, 'A dry sherry, please.'

'How very proper of you.'

His teasing smile made her heart lurch. 'I happen to like dry sherry.' She was aware she sounded defensive.

'If I remember rightly, you used to prefer a cocktail— something more laid-back and exotic.'

Refusing to let his mockery throw her, she said coolly, 'My tastes have altered since then. Of course, if you haven't *got* any dry sherry…'

'Don't worry, I'm quite sure I can provide anything you want.'

Trying to ignore the mocking gleam in his eye, she asked, 'I don't suppose there were any messages?'

Lifting the decanter, he filled two sherry glasses with the pale amber liquid and handed her one, before answering, 'None. Which isn't like Melinda. Though she's seldom, if ever, on time, she usually manages to keep in touch. If for some reason she's changed her mind and decided not to come until tomorrow, I'm surprised she hasn't let me know.'

'Can't you phone her?' Fran asked practically.

'Before I went up to shower I tried calling her hotel, but she wasn't in her room. The receptionist on the desk told me she'd gone out, after a phone call from a man.'

Drily, he added, 'If I didn't know how attached she is to the good life, I might be worried.'

'But you're not?'

Blaze shook his head. 'Money can buy pretty well any-thing. Including a faithful wife.'

His chiselled lips twisted into a smile. 'Now you're go-ing to say money can't buy love, but if you remember I did qualify it by saying *pretty well* anything. I'm under no illusions that Melinda loves me. I don't want her to.

'As I've said before, what I *do* want is a beautiful, passionate lover, a good-tempered, stimulating companion, and a mother for my children. She's willing to be all of those in return for a life of luxury...'

His eyes narrowed on Fran's transparent face. 'You seem to have some grave misgivings?'

She bit her lip, and, fighting down the impulse to tell him what Melinda had said about children, sidestepped the issue. 'It's really none of my business. The only thing that concerns me is that you and Miss Ross should be satisfied with my work.'

'I'm sure she will be...'

As he finished speaking, the young maid appeared to announce that dinner was ready.

Blaze nodded. 'We'll be in directly. Oh, and Hannah, please see that the doors to the living room and the dining room are left open.'

She gave a little bob of acknowledgement, and departed.

Turning to Fran, Blaze relieved her of her glass, and, before she could attempt to argue, stooped and lifted her with what seemed to be effortless ease.

'I'm sure you *could* make it on foot, but we don't want the soup to get cold, do we?'

Her heart seemed to miss a beat, and, made breathless by the strength of his arms and the contact with his muscular body, she made no attempt to answer.

As he carried her through the hall Mortimer appeared. Just for an instant the butler's face registered surprise.

'Miss Holt has ricked her ankle,' Blaze paused to explain blandly.

Something about the way he spoke, a hint of amusement in that deep, attractive voice rattled her even further. A quick glance at her tormentor convinced Fran he was *enjoying* himself. Hot and angry, she clenched her teeth.

'Indeed, sir? Most regrettable.' Mortimer shook his head gravely.

Carrying her through to the beautiful oak-panelled dining room, lit only by candles, Blaze set her on her feet with care, supporting her with one arm while he pulled out her chair.

'Thank you,' she said stiffly.

'My pleasure.' He smiled at her, a smile that despite its mockery held an irresistible charm.

Distracted, she sat down incautiously and winced.

He raised a questioning brow.

'A bruised hip,' she admitted.

'I see your arm's badly bruised too. A result of the bag-snatching incident?'

'Yes.'

When she was settled comfortably, he took his own place at the head of the long table. It was set with superb porcelain, fine crystal, fresh flowers and candelabra, and could easily have seated twenty.

The meal that followed was excellent, but, in spite of having had nothing but a sandwich at lunchtime, with so much on her mind Fran found herself unable to enjoy it.

On edge and anxious, aware that Blaze watched her like a hawk, she sipped the light white wine, which was pleasantly cool and refreshing, and made a pretence of eating.

Her companion wasn't fooled for an instant. 'Why don't you stop worrying about Varley?'

Grey-green eyes met charcoal-grey with a mixture of distress and defiance. 'How can I help but worry when I don't know what's happened to him...?'

'He doesn't seem to be worried about you. In spite of the fact that you were doing his dirty work...'

Fran set down her fork with a sharp click.

Blaze shrugged. 'Okay, I'll rephrase that. Though *you* were taking all the responsibility, he hasn't even rung to make sure you got here safely.'

'That's one of the reasons that makes me think he may have had an accident. He could be badly injured, lying unconscious in some hospital.'

Candlelight reflected in his dark eyes, Blaze said dismissively, 'He *could* be, but I think it unlikely. In fact I'd wager that you're the one who's come off worst, being attacked like that.'

Since seeing her bruised arm he seemed to be taking the whole thing a great deal more seriously.

Truthfully, she said, 'My main concern was always the necklace.'

The butler approached and cleared his throat discreetly.

Blaze glanced up. 'Yes, what is it, Mortimer?'

'A telephone call, sir. I wouldn't have interrupted your meal, but the gentleman, who failed to give his name, insisted that it was urgent.'

Judging by the butler's offended air, Blaze felt sure that 'failed' was a euphemism for 'refused'.

Tossing down his napkin, he rose to his feet and, turning to Fran, said, 'If you'll excuse me?'

Her heart beating faster with a combination of alarm, hope and excitement, she watched him follow the butler from the room.

CHAPTER FOUR

AFTER perhaps a couple of minutes Blaze returned and resumed his seat, his hard-boned, attractive face unreadable.

In answer to Fran's anxious glance, he shook his head. 'It was neither Melinda nor Varley, I'm afraid. Merely business.'

'Oh.' Disappointment clouded the clear greeny-grey eyes.

He refilled her glass, and, taking up the conversation where they'd left off, remarked, 'Even though the necklace was safe, the fact that the attack happened at all must have left you pretty badly shaken.'

'My confidence was,' she admitted. 'That's why I didn't want to report the incident and risk having to hang about. Though the man who helped me up—' All at once she remembered the 'colonel', and stopped abruptly. 'Or should I say *Mr Bellamy*?'

Blaze grimaced ruefully. 'So you recognised him? When I discovered you'd seen the taxi, I wondered if you might have done.'

'Then his coming to Balantyne Hall wasn't a coincidence?'

'No, it wasn't a coincidence.'

Light beginning to dawn, she said slowly, 'He was on the same Manchester to London plane as myself.'

'He belongs to Ritters. I hired him to keep an eye on you,' Blaze admitted coolly.

A private detective! Her blood ran cold. The thought of being followed and spied on was an unpleasant one, to say the least.

'He was most concerned about the attack,' Blaze went on. 'He felt that, knowing what he did know, he should have been able to prevent it... But, though he's an experienced man, an ex-police officer, he admits the suddenness took him by surprise.'

Fran's well-marked brows drew together in a frown. 'You said *knowing what he did know*... What did he know?'

'That he wasn't the only person tailing you.'

As she gazed at her companion blankly, Blaze went on, 'He described the other man as thin and nondescript-looking, with sandy hair and a sharp, ferrety face...'

Like someone in a dream, she added, 'His suit was creased and he carried a mac over his arm. *He* was on the same plane too...'

'So you spotted him?'

'While I was waiting by the reception desk I looked up and he seemed to be watching me... But then he walked away...'

Feeling as though she was caught up in some crazy *Alice in Wonderland* situation, Fran asked almost pleadingly, 'Are you *sure* he was following me? It doesn't make sense...'

'It does if he knew you were carrying the necklace.'

'No one could possibly have known.'

'Someone did.'

'You mean the theft of my handbag? But surely that was just petty crime? The sort of thing that happens every day?'

'According to Bellamy, most people who commit petty crime are opportunists. On the face of it, this man tailed you all the way from Manchester to do it.'

'What makes you think it was him?'

'It seems logical... Could it have been him?'

Doubtfully, she said, 'It *could* have, I suppose. Though I certainly couldn't swear to it. Everything happened so quickly that the whole thing was just a blur... Didn't Mr Bellamy get a glimpse of whoever it was?'

'Unfortunately not. He was looking to see if there was another taxi coming—'

'To enable him to follow me?'

'Ironic, isn't it?'

She harked back. 'But if it *was* this man, why bother to tail me to London? Why not do the job at Manchester airport?'

'Too close to home, perhaps... Or simply to throw us off the scent by making it look like petty crime.'

Fran shook her head. 'It sounds so *far-fetched*...'

'You know the old saying about truth being stranger than fiction...'

There was a pause in the conversation while the main course dishes were cleared.

When Fran refused the sweet, Blaze too waved it away, and suggested, 'Shall we have coffee on the terrace?'

Rising to his feet, he stood by her chair, looking down at her.

Recalling the way he'd carried her here, the effect it had had on her, she went hot all over. 'I don't need any help. I can walk perfectly well.'

'Don't be a fool,' Blaze said shortly. 'You'll only chance making it worse.'

'I don't want you to carry me,' she insisted, a note of near-panic creeping into her voice.

Mortimer, who had appeared as if by magic, cleared his throat and addressed his master. 'If I might be permitted to suggest a solution, sir?'

'*You'll* carry Miss Holt?' Blaze asked flippantly.

'That was not what I had in mind, sir.' The butler's response to his master's levity held the merest suggestion of dignified reproof.

'Then what did you have in mind, Mortimer?'

'It occurred to me, sir, that the late master's chair might be pressed into service. Towards the end of his life Sir Edward found it more suitable than an ordinary dining chair.'

The butler signalled to one of the footmen, who pushed forward a compact, leather-covered chair with neat arms: a chair that moved easily on castors.

Turning to Fran, Blaze raised an eyebrow. 'Well? Which is it to be?'

'The chair will do fine, thank you.'

'Then allow me, miss.' The butler offered her a black-clad arm and, when she had changed seats, made himself personally responsible for pushing the chair through to the living room and out on to the terrace.

'Thank you, Mortimer.' She was sincerely grateful. 'That was an absolute brainwave.'

Looking gratified, the butler bowed, and withdrew.

'Now, why do I get the feeling that Mortimer, who is a self-confessed misogynist, is on your side?' Blaze asked ironically.

Remembering his earlier remark about her being too sassy, she bit back the rejoinder on the tip of her tongue and said sweetly, 'I really can't imagine.'

He darted her a sharp glance, but let it go.

Beyond the lighted terrace it was quite dark now; the sky was like black velvet and the stars looked even brighter.

An exotic scent compounded of flowers and lemon and spice hung on the still air, and the night had turned so hot and sultry they could have been in the tropics rather than the English countryside.

There was a faint rattle and the maid appeared with a tray of coffee. Putting it carefully on the table, she asked, 'Shall I pour, sir?'

'No, thank you, Hannah, we'll help ourselves.'

When the girl had gone, Blaze offered Fran a hand. 'If

you move to one of the loungers you'll be able to put your foot up.'

Ignoring the proffered hand, she said shortly, 'Thank you, but I'm quite comfortable where I am.'

He gave a slight shrug, before asking, 'Would you like a brandy or a liqueur?'

'No, thank you, just coffee.'

He poured, and passed her a cup. 'A little cream, no sugar.'

'Thank you.' She felt a secret frisson of pleasure that after three years he still remembered how she liked her coffee.

Pouring his own, which he always took black and sugarless, he remarked, 'You don't *look* particularly comfortable. Sure you don't want to move?'

'I hardly think it's worth it,' she refused coolly. 'I'd like to go to bed as soon as I've finished my coffee.'

Lifting a dark brow, Blaze queried, 'Do I detect a touch of frost in the air?'

Her indignation surfaced in a rush. 'You surely don't expect me to *like* the fact that you had me spied on as though I were some criminal?'

'No,' he admitted. 'But I did what I thought was necessary.'

'How long has he been watching me?'

'Since I got word of Varley's financial problems and began to smell a rat.'

'So that's how you knew I wasn't living at Kirk's apartment...' A further and equally disagreeable thought struck her. 'I suppose you were having *him* followed too?

'No, wait... That doesn't make sense... If you *had* been you would have known where he was and what he was doing.'

Blaze smiled mirthlessly. 'I *should* have known. But whether by chance or design—you see, I'm prepared to give him the benefit of the doubt—your fiancé managed to lose the man who was shadowing him.'

'Before or after he reached Amsterdam?'

'He didn't go to Amsterdam.'

'Of course he went to Amsterdam. I saw him off at the airport myself.'

'You might have gone as far as Departures with him and kissed him goodbye…in fact I know you did. But he didn't get on the plane for Amsterdam. As soon as you had disappeared into the crowd he doubled back. He was heading *out* of the airport when he gave my detective the slip.'

'I thought you were giving him the benefit of the doubt?' she observed acidly.

'Very well. He was heading *out* of the airport when my detective lost him. Have you any idea why he changed his mind?'

'I don't believe he did,' she denied stoutly. 'The agency you hired doesn't seem to be particularly competent. Are you sure your so-called detective was following the right man?'

'He was following the man you'd just said goodbye to. A man he described as being of medium height, slim build, blond and good-looking, in his early thirties. It tallies perfectly with your own description.'

'Yes, but…' She shook her head as if to clear it. 'There *must* be some mistake. The Amsterdam trip was very important. Kirk would never have changed his mind at the last minute… And if he had why didn't he come back to the shop?'

'That's fairly obvious. Because he didn't want *you* to know he hadn't gone. He wanted you to stick to the plan. Which you did…'

Suddenly bold, she carried the war into the enemy camp. 'Well, as I did, and as you have your necklace safely back, whatever Kirk did or didn't do—and I don't for an instant believe your detective's absurd story—it's really none of your business. You've attacked both his reputation and his integrity, you've accused him of gambling and of planning to steal your precious rubies, and now I think you...' Running out of breath, she stopped short.

'Owe him an apology?' Blaze suggested.

'Yes.'

'Then when he gets here I'll give him one. What about you?'

'Me?'

'Wouldn't you say I also owe *you* an apology?'

She smiled derisively. 'For thinking I would be willing to bolt to South America and join a jewel thief on the run? It was too funny to take seriously.'

A glint in his eye, he said, 'I'm glad you were amused. But I still feel I should make amends. After all, we were once...' the pause was infinitesimal '...good friends.'

Something about the way he was looking at her mouth raised all the tiny hairs on the back of her neck.

Setting her coffee cup down on the table with a little crash, she stammered, 'R-really, there's no need to apologise...'

Then, in an effort to deflect an intention that was almost palpable, she rose to her feet, adding hastily, 'If you don't mind I'd like to go to bed now. It's been a tiring day... If Kirk comes after I've gone—'

'Mortimer will no doubt let him in.'

'Then I'll say goodnight.'

'I'll see you up. I don't intend to be too late myself.' A strange note in his voice, he added, 'Tomorrow looks like being a busy day.'

To Fran's consternation he stooped, and, one arm beneath her knees, the other supporting her back, lifted her as though she were a feather.

Swallowing, she tried hard to appear unconcerned, but

every nerve in her body had tightened in fright and her pulses were racing madly.

He looked at her, his dark eyes gleaming between long, thick lashes, and suggested, 'It would make it a lot easier if you were to put your arms around my neck.'

As she held back, he said encouragingly, 'It's not difficult. You've done it before.'

Damn him! she thought angrily. He was deliberately tormenting her. But circumstances had given him the upper hand, and there was no point in engaging in a verbal battle. Particularly as she had little chance of winning. She was well aware, from past experience, that both his wit and his tongue were quicker than her own.

Biting her lip, she slid her arms around his neck and clasped her hands together. Her fingers brushed the short hair that curled slightly into his nape and her heart lurched.

'That's better,' he said softly. 'I always did like a bit of co-operation.'

From the corner of her eye she saw that his handsome face wore a look of seraphic innocence obviously intended to infuriate her.

Well, she wouldn't rise to the bait.

Determinedly changing the subject, she remarked, 'You mentioned a busy day tomorrow. Have you many guests arriving? I mean for the weekend.'

Crossing the living room, he headed for the stairs before answering, 'About forty people in all. One or two old cronies of my father's, the others either neighbours or business acquaintances and their wives, none of whom are staying the night.'

She was surprised. 'Oh? I thought it was to be a weekend house party for close friends and family?'

'The only family I have left live in the States. So do most of my friends. The same goes for Melinda...'

Though he was talking while he carried her up the stairs

he showed no sign of being out of breath, and she mar-
velled at his fitness.

'I would have preferred to have kept everything under
wraps until we were married, but Melinda wanted a formal
engagement party. She couldn't wait to meet some of my
aristocratic neighbours and show off both the necklace and
its designer...'

Fran had wondered why, knowing quite well who she
was, Blaze had invited her. The answer seemed to be that
Melinda had wanted her.

'Afterwards, when both the wedding and the honeymoon
were safely over, the plan was to hold a big party at the
New York Plaza.'

It occurred to Fran that he was using the past tense, as
if Melinda's absence had somehow altered things, made
him change his mind.

But he wouldn't change his mind just because his fiancée, whom he'd admitted was usually late, hadn't yet arrived...

Fran's train of thought came to an abrupt halt as she
realised that they had almost reached her room.

Eager to escape, she was already rehearsing a cool,
Thank you, and goodnight, when he stopped at her door.

But, instead of setting her on her feet, as she'd expected,
he advised, 'Hang on,' and, bending a little to turn the
knob, walked straight in, shouldering the door shut behind
him.

She was suddenly scared stiff, not so much of *him*, but
of her own reactions to him.

Her voice, normally low and attractively husky, was now
high and a trifle shrill as she demanded, 'What are you
doing?'

He raised a dark brow at her tone. 'What does it look as
if I'm doing?'

Masking her fear with anger, she told him curtly, 'I'd rather you didn't come into my room.'

'It occurred to me that you might need some help.'

'I don't need any help. I can manage perfectly well...'

He was still standing holding her, as though he was enjoying the feel of her slender body resting against his.

'So if you'll put me down...' she added icily.

'Certainly.' Crossing the polished floorboards, he laid her on the bed and sat on the edge, trapping her there.

Whoever had drawn the curtains and turned back the covers had left the bedside lamp on, and while she lay in a circle of light his face was in shadow.

'Happier now?' he queried silkily.

She was anything but.

The fact that she was lying down while he was sitting upright put her at a grave disadvantage.

Gritting her teeth, she made an attempt to push herself into a sitting position.

He prevented her by the simple expedient of pulling her elbows from beneath her.

Falling back with a gasp, she stared at him wide-eyed, the lamp casting the shadow of her long lashes on to her cheeks.

His face looked set and grim, and, dropping the façade of anger, she whispered, 'Please, Blaze, let me get up.'

'That's better,' he observed with satisfaction. 'I like a woman to have some spirit, but I also like her to have some manners.'

'I—I'm sorry... I was...'

'Scared?'

Her silence was answer enough.

'There's no need to be.'

'Thank the Lord for that,' she exclaimed fervently.

He laughed, breaking the tension.

Relaxing a fraction, she asked carefully, 'Please will you let me get up?'

'When I'm good and ready.' Seeing her lose colour, he added, 'Don't worry, I promise I'm not planning to ravish you while your fiancé's back's turned.'

Her lashes flickered. 'Then what are you planning?'

'Just to collect on the bet I won.'

She found herself begging, 'Please don't kiss me.'

'I wasn't going to,' he said coolly. 'The bet was that if Varley wasn't back *you* would kiss *me*.'

'Making that kind of bet is childish,' she muttered.

'Strange, I hadn't figured you as a welsher.'

Seeing, by his calm air of purpose, that he had no intention of letting her get away with it, she gave in. 'All right... But I'd like to sit up first.'

'You feel safer that way?'

Ignoring the taunt, she began to push herself upright.

This time he let her.

When they were face to face she hesitated, half hoping he would make the first move, but he just waited quietly.

She found herself looking at his firm, beautifully chiselled mouth. The top lip was a shade austere, the bottom one fuller, with a touch of sensuality.

It had always made butterflies flutter in her stomach. They were doing it now.

But she didn't need to kiss his mouth.

Tearing her eyes away, and telling herself she must get it over with, she leaned forward and kissed him.

She had meant to lightly brush his cheek, but without conscious volition her lips found his and lingered, unable to move away.

For a second or two he sat quiescent, then his own lips parted in response, deepening the kiss, adding fire and excitement and a drugging sweetness.

Her eyes closed and her arms went around his neck.

One of his hands moved to cup her nape, while the other found the curve of her breast and lovingly coaxed the nipple into life, before grazing over her slim waist, hip and thigh.

When he slipped the thin straps from her shoulders and eased down the bodice of her dress, she made no effort to prevent him.

Indeed, she would have helped him had it been necessary. But he was both experienced and skilful, with a touch that was as sure as it was delicate.

She was lying down now, her eyes tightly closed, shuddering as his lips explored the warm swell of her breasts.

There was nothing in the world but this man, and the way he was making her feel. She waited in an agony of need until his mouth closed on one waiting peak, causing needle-sharp stabs of ecstasy, a delight so pure it was almost pain.

At the same time his hand was stroking the warm silky skin of her inner thigh, slowly but surely travelling higher, making a pool of liquid heat form in the pit of her stomach.

A leisurely, unhurried lover, he had in the past made her wait, wringing from her sensations so exquisite that she had thought she could feel no more. Only to find, in the final act of love, that they had been merely the prelude...

When those questing fingers found the smooth satin of her briefs she gave a little murmur, a cross between a moan and a sigh.

He paused and drew back.

For an endless moment she waited, then she felt the mattress spring into place as his weight lifted from the edge. Dimly she realised he would be stripping off his clothes so he could join her.

It took a little while to dawn on her that there was no sound, no movement, just utter stillness.

Dazed and unbelieving, she opened her eyes to find he

was still fully dressed, standing motionless, staring down at her, his face in shadow.

'About time to call a halt, I think...' His voice sounded cool, almost casual, but his quickened breathing suggested that he wasn't quite as unmoved as he was making out. 'Otherwise I'll end up doing what I promised I wouldn't do...'

His words were like a deluge of icy water. Feeling sick, she sat up and dragged her bodice into place with unsteady hands.

He walked to the door and, his hand on the knob, turned to say, 'If Varley arrives in the next half-hour shall I send him along?'

She bit her lip until she tasted blood.

'I'm sorry,' he apologised immediately. 'That was unnecessarily cruel.'

A second later the door clicked to behind him.

Trembling all over, full of conflicting emotions, the chief of which was shame, she struggled to her feet and hobbled into the bathroom.

While she cleaned her teeth and prepared for bed with hands that shook so much they could hardly complete their task, she mentally flayed herself.

How *could* she have behaved like that? How *could* she have forgotten they were both engaged to marry someone else?

But she had. Rings and promises, rights and wrongs, other people had simply ceased to exist. The only thing that had mattered in the whole world had been *him*... Feeling his mouth on hers, his touch on her eager body...

If only he hadn't carried her upstairs... If only he hadn't insisted on her kissing him...

No, there was no way she could lay the blame at *his* door. If she had just kissed him with cool dismissiveness, he would have left it at that...

But she hadn't. She had kissed him with a longing that must have been manifest. *She* had been the instigator, and if he hadn't drawn back when he had she would have been guilty of sleeping with another woman's fiancé. And this time she couldn't say she hadn't known.

She would also have been guilty of cheating on her own fiancé...

Loving Kirk, as she did, how could she have wanted Blaze so much? Was she really so sex-starved? she wondered bitterly, until a little voice reminded her that what she had shared with Blaze in the past had never been just sex. She had loved him.

Now she loved Kirk.

Or did she? If she *really* loved him, how was it Blaze still had so much power over her?

As though the scales had fallen from her eyes she saw that if she had thought herself in love it had been with love itself, rather than with Kirk.

He was the first man, since Blaze, who had attracted her, and she had practically willed herself to love him.

She was almost twenty-seven. Perhaps her biological clock had been to blame, urging her to marry the first prepossessing male who came along, so enabling her to have the family she'd always wanted while she was still young.

Kirk was handsome and intelligent, considerate and charming, everything a woman could ask for in a husband. But she knew with a sudden clear insight that if he turned his back on her tomorrow he wouldn't break her heart, as Blaze had done.

Blaze had been her first love. *Her only love.* His mouth against hers like a drink of fresh water to someone dying of thirst. Her mouth against his a reaffirmation of her love, a love that had never really died.

The implications of that simple fact made her feel hollow

inside as she closed the bathroom door behind her and climbed into bed.

Blaze would doubtless go ahead as planned and marry Melinda Ross, but, aware of her true feelings, there was no way she could marry Kirk.

Lifting her hand, she looked at the ring he had slipped on to her finger. The ring Blaze had jeered at. The ring she had been so pleased with.

Then, knowing she couldn't go on wearing it, she took it off without a single pang of regret and put it on the bedside table.

When this weekend was over, instead of moving in with him she would have to find some other place to live, and in all probability another job. She couldn't imagine that he would want her around the place after she had broken their engagement.

Fate was strange. If Blaze hadn't invited them to Balantyne Hall, and Kirk hadn't insisted on accepting, none of this would have happened.

She would have continued to believe herself in love and been happy to look forward to a safe, settled future.

As it was, her whole life had been turned topsy-turvy, leaving her desolate and homeless, like the victim of some disaster.

For the second time in three years.

And from the same cause.

Still, she was a survivor, she told herself with a flash of spirit. She had rebuilt her life once. She could do it again.

But there wasn't only herself to take into account this time, she realised, reaching to switch off the bedside lamp. There was Kirk. How much would breaking their engagement upset him?

Not overmuch, if the stories of other women in his life had a grain of truth in them.

No, of course they hadn't. She just couldn't believe it.

From some of the things Blaze himself had admitted the detective agency had proved to be inefficient, to say the least. In all probability they had been investigating the wrong man.

And following the wrong man? Could they really have bungled the job *so* badly? The description had fitted to perfection...

But if it *had* been Kirk why had he changed his mind about going to Amsterdam? And if he had changed his mind, why hadn't he let her know? Why had he allowed her to wait for him at the airport? And why had he left that sketchy message at the information desk?

There were so many questions. All of which would have to remain unanswered, at least until Kirk himself turned up.

Which immediately posed a further set of questions. Where could he have got to? What was keeping him? Why hadn't he been in touch?

So many strange things had happened, including the theft of her handbag. Could that really have been carefully planned, as Blaze had suggested...?

Doing her best to push away the futile questions crowding in, Fran closed her eyes and tried to sleep. But, though weary, her brain refused to switch off.

It was dawn before she finally slipped into an uneasy doze, and her last unhappy thought was of Blaze. He was going to marry a woman he didn't love and who didn't love him, a woman who had made it plain that she had no intention of having his children...

A tap on the door disturbed her. Still half asleep, she called, 'Who is it?'

'Hannah, miss.'

'Come in.' Endeavouring to pull herself together, Fran struggled into a sitting position as the young maid carried in a tray of tea.

Putting the tray down on the bedside table, Hannah went to draw back the curtains.

The sky looked heavy, and the air coming through the open windows was as hot and humid as ever. Low on the horizon a bank of dark thunderclouds warned of an impending storm.

Wondering if it could be an omen, Fran shivered.

Peering blearily at her watch, she saw the hands stood at twelve fifteen. 'Good heavens!' she exclaimed. 'Is it really that time? Why didn't you wake me sooner?'

'The master gave instructions that if you seemed to be sleeping you weren't to be disturbed before noon, miss.'

'Is Mr Varley here yet, do you know?'

'No, miss, there've been no visitors.'

'What about Miss Ross? Has she arrived?'

'No, miss.'

With a growing feeling of hopelessness, Fran asked, 'Have there been any messages?'

'Not that I know of, miss.'

It seemed that nothing had changed, Fran thought almost despairingly.

'But Mr Mortimer would be the one to ask... Will that be all, miss?'

'Yes, thank you, Hannah.'

When the door had closed behind the maid, Fran poured herself some tea and drank it gratefully.

Despite sleeping late she felt headachy and unrefreshed, unwilling to face yet more waiting.

There was a phone at the bedside, and, picking up the receiver, she tapped in the number of Kirk's apartment, only to get the answering machine.

But what else had she expected? she asked herself crossly. She hadn't imagined for one minute that he'd actually be sitting at home. It was just a case of leaving no stone unturned.

Her next and only hope was William Bailey. He lived in the small flat above Varley's business premises, and had done since Kirk's father died. If there *had* been an accident of some kind he might be the one to know.

'William Bailey...' He answered on the third ring, in the dry, precise way she knew of old.

'William, it's Francesca Holt...'

Her good temper and pleasant manners had made her a firm favourite, and his tone was avuncular as he asked, 'What can I do for you, Francesca, my dear?'

'Have you heard anything of Kirk, by any chance?'

'I had a call from him first thing this morning.'

'Do you know where he is?' she asked eagerly.

Sounding puzzled, William said, 'I thought he was at Balantyne Hall with you.'

'No, he...he was held up and hasn't arrived yet. I wondered if he might have had an accident.'

'He sounded fine when I spoke to him.'

'What did he say?'

'Only that he looked like being away longer than he'd anticipated, and he wanted me to take charge of everything until I heard from him again.' Then, with sudden anxiety, 'Is there something wrong? You *are* at Balantyne Hall?'

'Yes.'

'And you've delivered the package safely?'

'Yes.'

She heard his sigh of relief, before he asked, 'But surely Kirk's been in touch with you?'

Remembering what the maid had said about Mortimer being the one to ask about messages, she said, 'It's all right, he's probably left a message. I'm sorry to have bothered you.'

'It was no bother, my dear. Have a pleasant weekend.'

CHAPTER FIVE

FRAN got out of bed, and, finding her ankle was a great deal better, headed for the bathroom, her thoughts racing.

If Kirk had told William that he might be away longer than he'd anticipated, something totally unexpected must have cropped up. Something of importance.

But what could have been of more importance than the safe delivery of the necklace and the weekend at Balantyne Hall?

Though she was very relieved that Kirk was at least safe, and not lying badly injured in some hospital, she was starting to feel annoyed and resentful that he hadn't let *her* know what was happening.

Unless there was a message.

Or perhaps by now he'd talked to Blaze?

As quickly as possible, she showered, put on a light cotton dress and a pair of low-heeled sandals, and, leaving her hair loose around her shoulders, made her way down the stairs.

Just as she reached the bottom, the butler appeared and enquired gravely, 'I trust the ankle is somewhat improved today, miss?'

She smiled at him. 'Much improved, thank you, Mortimer.'

'I'm pleased to hear you say so, miss.'

'Is there a message for me, from Mr Varley?'

'No, miss.'

'But he did phone?'

'Not to my knowledge, miss. Unless the master took the call.'

'Thank you, Mortimer. I'll ask him.'

'That won't be possible at the moment, miss. The master went out shortly after breakfast.'

Blaze knew quite well how worried and anxious she'd been; if he *had* heard from Kirk she couldn't believe that he would have left the house without setting her mind at rest.

Her silky brows drawing together in a frown, she asked, 'Do you happen to know where he went?'

'I understand he was going to town, miss.'

No doubt to find out what had delayed Melinda Ross. 'Did he say when he'd be home?'

'No, miss. He did say, however, that if he wasn't back for one o'clock you were to go ahead and have lunch without him.'

At that precise moment the grandfather clock whirred self-importantly and struck one.

'As it appears that you'll be lunching alone,' the butler went on in measured tones, 'if you would prefer to have lunch on the terrace, rather than in the dining room...?'

Neither prospect appealed.

Convinced now that, for whatever reason, Kirk wasn't going to come, and unable to bear the thought of just waiting around until Blaze and his fiancée returned, Fran found herself suddenly desperate to get away.

Her job was done. She had delivered the necklace, so what was there to stay for? Certainly not the party. It would be a form of torture to stand by and watch Blaze with his arm around Melinda Ross, introducing her as his bride-to-be.

And in the circumstances it was hardly fair to the other woman. If Melinda had had the faintest idea that in the past she and Blaze had been lovers, she would never have been invited.

Making up her mind in a rush, Fran said steadily, 'Thank

you, Mortimer, but I won't be staying for lunch. While I go up and pack my things, perhaps you'll be kind enough to—'

Recalling the theft of her bag, she stopped speaking abruptly. Oh, Lord, what on earth was she to do? She had no money and no credit cards.

There was money in her bank account, of course, but it was Saturday; the banks would be closed and her bank cards had disappeared along with everything else.

To add to her troubles, expecting to fly back with Kirk she had booked only a one-way ticket, so she had no means of getting back to Manchester.

And no home to go to if she got there.

She resolutely pushed that less than comforting thought away.

If she could get to London and book into a hotel for the night she could always explain the situation to William Bailey, and ask for his help.

'I'm sorry,' she said to the butler, who, head slightly bent, was waiting patiently. 'I was going to ask you to call me a taxi, but on the way here I had my bag stolen.'

'The master mentioned it,' Mortimer informed her gravely. 'It must have been very distressing, miss.'

'It's proving to be very inconvenient,' she remarked with feeling. Then, taking the bull by the horns, 'Mortimer, could you possibly lend me the taxi fare to London?'

For the first time the butler appeared discomfited. Clearing his throat, he assured her, 'I would have been happy to, miss, had the master not issued specific instructions to the contrary.'

As she gaped at him, he added, 'My understanding is that the master wishes you to remain at the Hall until his return.'

Fran bit her lip. Then, her voice even, said, 'I see. Thank you, Mortimer.'

Looking relieved that she had taken it in such a ladylike fashion, he reminded her, 'About lunch, miss...?'

'Thank you, but I won't be having lunch.'

She couldn't eat a bite; it would choke her... And if Blaze thought he could keep her here when she wanted to leave, he had another think coming!

If she couldn't take a taxi there was nothing to prevent her *walking* out.

Unwilling to involve the staff, however, she said carefully, 'When the master gets back, perhaps you'll be good enough to tell him I'm in my room?'

'Certainly, miss.' Mortimer inclined his head.

Her back ramrod-straight, a flag of colour flying in each cheek, Fran went up the stairs, her thoughts racing.

It couldn't be more than a mile or so to the main entrance, which was manned. And on her way here, just before the taxi had turned off by the stand of beeches, she remembered noticing a country hotel called The Mulberries. She would almost certainly be able to stay the night there.

As soon as the door of her room had closed behind her she gathered her belongings together, and, anger and the need for haste making her reckless, bundled them into her case anyhow and zipped up the lid.

She was about to hurry from the room when she recalled that Kirk's ring was still lying on the bedside table. Having nowhere to put it, she picked it up and thrust it back on to her finger.

Then, case in hand, she descended the stairs, praying she would meet no one. It was lunchtime, so with a bit of luck all the servants would either be eating or making preparations for the party.

Fate was on her side, and she was able to quietly open the heavy front door and let herself out without seeing a soul.

There wasn't a breath of air. Everything was so still that all of nature seemed to be holding its breath, waiting for the gathering storm to finally break.

Hopefully it would hold off until she reached the hotel, but she would have to hurry. Already thunder was rumbling in the distance, and flashes of lightning lit the louring sky.

The heat was oppressive, and before she'd gone a quarter of a mile she was bathed in perspiration. Her case, which she had considered light, now seemed to weigh a ton, and her ankle, protesting at such cavalier treatment, had started to ache again.

Gritting her teeth, she kept going.

The gatehouse was in sight when the first heavy drops of rain began to plop on to the tarmac. She quickened her pace, while the air took on the familiar ozoney smell that rain settling on dust makes.

She was several hundred yards from the gates when there was a dazzling flash and a loud crack of thunder. Her ears were still ringing when the heavens opened and the rain poured down with such force that she reeled under the onslaught.

Instantly saturated, she put her head down and battled on while, almost overhead, it seemed, the lightning flashed and the thunder boomed like heavy gunfire.

Half blinded by the flashes and the deluge, and deafened by the noise of the thunder, she failed to either see or hear the car that was heading up the drive to the Hall, until it drew up alongside her.

Through the streaming windows she caught a glimpse of the driver, just as he leaned over and opened the passenger door. 'Get in,' Blaze ordered curtly.

Like hell! she thought rebelliously, and kept walking.

The next instant he had backed up and leapt out.

Guessing his intention, she made an effort to hold on to her case, but he took it from her as easily as one might take candy from a baby and slung it on to the back seat. Then, throwing a muscular arm around her, he bundled her into the car without ceremony, and slammed the door.

'How dare you manhandle me?' she spluttered, as he jumped in beside her.

'Fasten your seat belt,' he instructed tersely.

When she didn't immediately obey, he leaned over and, his face set and angry, fastened it for her.

'I don't want to go back,' she spat at him. 'I want to leave.'

Taking not the slightest bit of notice, he put his foot on the accelerator and they started up the drive, the wipers, though working at full speed, failing to clear the water cascading down the windscreen.

Though Blaze had only left the car for a matter of seconds he was soaked to the skin, his hair plastered seal-like to his head.

He hadn't been wearing a jacket, and his fine cotton shirt clung wetly to him, showing his biceps and the sprinkle of dark hair on his chest.

She took a quick, furtive glance at his face. Moisture beaded his lashes and drops of water trickled down his lean cheek and dripped off his chin.

When they reached the house, he drove round the side, through an archway, and drew into the old stable-block which served as garages.

'We can't get any wetter,' he remarked grimly, 'so we may as well save Donaldson a job and put the car away.'

When the Mercedes was safely under cover, he collected Fran's case and held open her door.

In mutinous silence she climbed out.

Putting his jacket around her, he hurried her from beneath the shelter of the overhanging eaves and across the gleaming cobblestones.

Miraculously, the heat had all been washed away and the

air was cool and fresh. Rain was still pelting down, pouring off the guttering, gurgling down the pipes, running in torrents along the drainage channels.

Opening an oak door on to a flagged passage, with a flight of stone steps at the end, he told her brusquely, 'It'll be quicker to go in this way and up the back stairs.'

Leaving a trail of wet footprints, and dripping copious amounts of water, they climbed the stairs to a landing with two archways. Blaze led her through the nearest, and they emerged into the gallery which ran the length of the house.

'Here we are.' He opened a door to the left and ushered her into a small, white-walled sitting room.

It was simply furnished with a polished bureau, several bookcases and a stereo unit. Two armchairs, a low settee and an oblong coffee table were grouped in front of a large stone fireplace.

Some kindling, a box of matches and a basket of logs suggested that during the winter months the fireplace was put to good use.

It must be really cosy then, Fran thought longingly. At the moment the casement windows were open wide and rain was beating in, pooling on the stone sills and running on to the plum-coloured carpet.

The air felt damp and distinctly cool, and, chilled to the bone, she found herself shivering as she glanced around the sitting room. It seemed to be part of a self-contained suite, with a bedroom at either end. But why should Blaze need his own suite?

As though reading her thoughts, he set her case down and, taking his wet jacket from around her shoulders, said trenchantly, 'I like to have some privacy.'

'I would have thought it was impossible to have any real privacy with a houseful of servants,' she commented a shade tartly.

'The servants only venture up here on my express instructions. They don't even come up to clean unless I ask them to.'

While he spoke he studied her with a kind of insolent appraisal, his head tilted a little to one side.

Her hair hung in dripping rats' tails around her pale face, and her thin cotton dress, turned almost transparent by the wet, was plastered to her.

His eyes on her breasts, he remarked silkily, 'You seem to be cold,' and smiled when she flushed.

Recognising that his anger had by no means diminished, she felt a rush of alarm and apprehension. Her skin goose-fleshed and she began to shiver in earnest.

He reached to close the windows, then, turning back to her, advised curtly, 'There are two bathrooms, so I suggest you make use of Melinda's and jump into a hot bath before you catch a chill.'

Not liking the idea of intruding on to his fiancée's terrain, but wanting to escape his nerve-racking gaze, Fran hurried over to the door he'd indicated.

She was halfway through it when he asked, 'By the way, have you had any lunch?'

'No.' She answered without turning round.

'Neither have I. I'll ask Hannah to bring up a pot of tea and some sandwiches for when you're through.'

Closing the door behind her, she found herself in a pleasant cream-carpeted bedroom. It could hardly have been called neat, however. Drawers had been pulled out and left, a lace negligee lay where it had fallen, and a discarded dress had been thrown carelessly over a chair.

A built-in wardrobe ran the length of one wall and its doors had been left open to display a range of clothes and accessories that, despite their disarray, would have been the envy of most females.

Feeling uncomfortable, and unwilling to linger in the

other woman's bedroom, Fran went quickly into the well-appointed bathroom.

Her mother, had she been alive to see it, would unhesitatingly have called it a tip.

A monogrammed robe lay where it had been tossed. Caps and lids had been left off the toothpaste and various other creams and lotions. Used facial wipes and tissues and a half-empty bottle of moisturiser, graced the sink, and several towels littered the floor.

There was, however, a supply of fresh towels piled neatly on a shelf, along with a selection of unopened toiletries. Fran took a towel and hung it over the rail, before stooping to put the plug in the bath and turn on the water.

She had just peeled off her sodden dress and undies when the door opened and Blaze walked in, still fully clothed.

Taken by surprise, she was slow to snatch the towel and cover her nakedness.

Noting the expression on her face, he said sardonically, 'There's no need to look quite so outraged.'

'You could have knocked,' she protested indignantly, looking anywhere but at him.

'I did. You probably couldn't hear for the water running... Don't worry,' he went on with contemptuous unconcern, 'it's no big deal. After all, I have seen you in the altogether before. In fact, if you remember, we once shared a shower.'

Remembering only too well, she went scarlet.

Getting under her guard, hacking at her defences, he added mockingly, 'At the time you were quite enthusiastic...'

'What do you want?' she demanded in a half-stifled voice, both hands holding the towel in place.

'I thought you might need this.'

She realised for the first time that he was carrying her case.

'Oh… Thank you… If you would just put it down?'

'Certainly.' Glancing around him, he grimaced at the mess, then, sounding slightly more human, said, 'I'm afraid Melinda isn't the tidiest of women. It's one of the reasons I agreed to separate rooms. Less aggro… And to be honest this is partly my fault. I omitted to ask one of the maids to come up. If you would prefer to use my bathroom…?'

'No, no, I wouldn't.' The bath was getting over-full, and, clutching the towel to her, she stooped to turn off the taps, adding jerkily, 'This will do fine, thank you.'

He grinned wryly at her determined politeness. 'Then I'll go and take a shower…' At the door he turned and cocked an eyebrow at her. 'Unless you want me to stay and wash your back?'

Losing her cool, she cried, 'No, I *don't* want you to stay and wash my back. I want you to get out of here and stay out.'

As he closed the door behind him and walked away she heard his soft, mocking laugh.

There had been anger rather than amusement beneath the mockery, and she was well aware that this attempt to harass and demean her had been quite intentional. He had wanted to pay her back.

Though for what? she wondered bleakly. For attempting to leave, when for some unknown reason he wanted her to stay?

Determined to take no more chances, she crossed to the door and turned the key in the lock before discarding the towel and stepping into the steaming tub.

Some twenty minutes later, dressed in a coffee-coloured two-piece—the least crumpled thing in her case—she made her way back to the sitting room.

Though outside the storm was still raging, inside it was comfortably warm and cosy.

Blaze, wearing casual trousers and an olive-green cotton-knit shirt, was lounging in one of the armchairs in front of a cheerful log fire.

His legs stretched out, his dark head resting against the back of the chair, he appeared to be half asleep, and she paused.

Noting her hesitation, he invited coolly, 'Do come and join me.'

Determined to appear calm and self-possessed, she sat down in the chair opposite while, lids drooping, he studied her through long, thick lashes.

Her newly washed ash-brown hair, still a little damp and curling slightly, was loose around her shoulders, and her nose was undeniably shiny.

She knew she must look a fright.

He thought she looked fresh and lovely and oddly vulnerable.

A tray with a selection of dainty sandwiches, home-made fruit cake and a pot of tea was waiting on the low table.

Drawing back his feet, he sat up and reached to pass her a napkin and a plate. 'Would you like—'

'I'd like to know why you insisted on me coming back to the Hall.'

His voice smooth and hard as polished granite, he said, 'Neither of us have had any lunch, and, according to Hannah, you didn't have any breakfast either, so I think we should eat first and talk later. Now, would you like to start with ham or cucumber?'

Realising it was useless to argue, Fran gave in with what grace she could muster. 'Cucumber, please.'

The sandwiches were delicious, and, all at once finding herself ravenous, she began to tuck in with a will.

They ate without speaking until the plates were empty and they had finished their second cups of tea. Then it was Blaze who broke the silence to ask, 'What made you decide to leave so suddenly?'

'I couldn't see any point in staying.'

The dark eyes pinned her. 'So you're not still expecting Varley to turn up?'

'No,' she admitted.

'Does that mean you've heard from him?'

She shook her head. 'I thought *you* might have done, until Mortimer told me you'd gone out.'

Blaze raised a dark brow.

A shade awkwardly, she explained, 'You knew how anxious I'd been; I didn't think you would have left without first putting my mind at rest…'

'I'm not noted for being kind to my adversaries.'

Startled, she asked, 'Is that how you regard me?'

'How else?'

'B-but I don't see why,' she stammered helplessly. 'I've tried to keep to the arrangements that were made.'

'I'm sure you have,' he said sardonically. 'I bet Varley's proud of you!'

When she just looked at him, Blaze said, ice in his voice, 'Don't tell me he didn't congratulate you on a job well done?'

'I told you, I haven't spoken to him… If *you* have—'

'I haven't,' Blaze denied shortly. 'Nor did I expect to. But when I found you were so anxious to get away I knew that he must have been in touch. So why not tell me the truth? Where were you planning to meet him?'

'You're quite wrong. He *hasn't* been in touch, and I *wasn't* planning to meet him.'

'You lie quite convincingly.'

'I'm not lying. Why should I lie?'

His voice like a whiplash, he asked, 'Then what made you decide to leave?'

'When Hannah told me Kirk still hadn't come and there were no messages, I tried ringing his apartment. All I got was the answer-machine…'

Seeing Blaze's lips twist, she shook her head. 'I hadn't *expected* him to be there; I just wanted to try every avenue possible.'

'Which did you try next?'

'I rang William Bailey on the offchance that he might have heard something. He lives over Varley's business premises, so I thought if there *had* been an accident of some kind...'

'What did Bailey have to say?'

'That he'd talked to Kirk first thing this morning, but he didn't know—'

His grey eyes narrowed on her face, Blaze broke in tersely, 'Perhaps you can tell me verbatim?'

Taking a deep breath, she repeated the telephone conversation word for word, as far as she could remember, ending, 'From what William said, I knew that something totally unexpected must have cropped up. Something that had been important enough to divert Kirk and—'

'And make him keep the whole thing a secret—not only from his right hand man but from his own fiancée?'

'That's what I can't understand,' she admitted.

'You used the word *divert...*'

'Well, I—'

'Without knowing any more, what made you decide there and then that he wasn't going to turn up at all?'

'I just felt instinctively that he—'

'My dear Francesca, you'll have to do a great deal better than that.'

Sighing, she insisted, 'It happens to be the truth... In any case, I was sick of all the waiting, and I'd started to feel angry and resentful that he hadn't been in touch.'

There was a moment's silence, then Blaze pursued, 'So you made up your mind to go?'

'Yes.'

'To run while my back was turned?'

Hearing the censure, she said defensively, 'Why not? I'd done my part.'

Just for an instant he looked so furious that she flinched. Then the anger was wiped away, and he asked evenly, 'Had you forgotten you'd been invited for the weekend?'

She licked her dry lips. 'As the whole thing had fallen through, I didn't want to stay on my own.'

'And I get the feeling that you hadn't wanted to come in the first place?'

'No, I hadn't.' She refused to lie.

'Why not? It couldn't have been because you knew *I* was Edward Balantyne.'

When she remained silent, he asked, 'Had Melinda said something to put you off?'

'No.' This time she was forced to lie, and judging by his expression he knew it.

Letting it go, however, he asked, 'When you did make up your mind to leave, what were your plans? If you weren't meeting Varley—'

'I've told you I wasn't.'

'Then what did you intend to do?'

'My first thought was to get to London and book into a hotel for the night, but—'

'You couldn't raise the taxi fare?'

'As well you know.'

'So you *did* ask Mortimer.' Blaze sounded wryly amused. 'I can just picture his face.'

'Go ahead and laugh, why don't you?'

Ignoring the bitterness, Blaze pursued, 'But you still went ahead and walked out. I take it you weren't planning to walk all the way to London?'

'No. There's a county hotel a few miles down the road. I was hoping to stay there.'

'Then what?'

'William Bailey would have helped me.'

'If you hadn't heard from Varley, why were you so desperate to go just at that minute?'

Watching the betraying colour rise in her cheeks, he said softly, 'I see. So this sudden urge to run was brought on by what happened last night.'

He was too close to the truth.

Forced into a corner, Fran lifted her chin and lied, 'I'm sorry about that. I was missing Kirk and wishing he was there...'

She had the satisfaction of seeing Blaze's jaw tighten with fury.

Pressing home her unexpected advantage, she added with studied nonchalance, 'It's just as well you didn't get...too involved. I suppose you were missing your fiancée too, and if we'd both lost our heads it could have caused problems.'

'It could indeed,' he agreed trenchantly. 'Though Melinda is easygoing, I don't think she would have been too happy. Especially in view of our past association...'

'That's why I thought it would be better if I left before she got here.'

'I fail to see what difference it makes,' Blaze said, showing an apparent insensitivity quite foreign to his nature. 'That is unless you were intending to tell her everything.'

'I wasn't intending to tell her anything,' Fran denied sharply. 'But in the circumstances I didn't feel comfortable about staying, and I still think it would be best if I left before she gets here.'

'Tell me,' he asked silkily, 'is the imminent arrival of my fiancée the only reason you want to leave?'

'Is it imminent?'

He shrugged. 'As I haven't spoken to her, I can't say for certain, though I'm beginning to doubt it.'

'But when Mortimer said you'd gone to London, I thought you'd be sure to see her.'

'I called at her hotel, but she'd checked out and her car was no longer there.'

'Then she's probably on her way here now.'

'If she's *still* on her way she must have gone via Scotland.' At Fran's startled glance, he explained, 'She checked out last night. About an hour after I rang.'

'I suppose...' Fran stopped and bit her lip.

He read the unspoken thought with ease, and told her calmly, 'I considered that possibility, so I contacted the police and gave them all the necessary details. There'd been no reported accident involving a car and driver of that description.'

Leaning forward, he threw another log on the fire before remarking, 'So it's anyone's guess where she's got to.'

'There may be a message.'

'There's no message. I checked with Mortimer before getting into the shower.' Frowning, he added, 'And with only an hour or so to go before the party I would have expected her to be here, if she's going to come.'

Blaze's mention of the party roused Fran to action. There was no point in her sitting here discussing his fiancée's absence. In all probability Melinda would turn up any minute, and everything would proceed as planned.

But hopefully without *her*.

Striving to sound matter-of-fact, Fran said, 'I'm quite sure Miss Ross won't miss her own party... But in any event *I* don't intend to stay.'

When Blaze said nothing, she announced with more assurance than she felt, 'In fact I *insist* on leaving.'

Something in his face, his continued silence, scared her stiff. 'You can't keep me here against my will,' she cried.

'How melodramatic,' he mocked.

'But you *can't*.'

His lean cheeks creased in a smile. 'Don't bet on it.' Then, calmly, 'A moment ago I asked if the arrival of my

Play **LUCKY HEARTS** for this...

exciting FREE gift!
**This surprise mystery gift
could be yours free**

when you play **LUCKY HEARTS!**
...then continue your lucky streak
with a sweetheart of a deal!

1. Play Lucky Hearts as instructed on the opposite page.
2. Send back this card and you'll receive 2 brand-new Harlequin Presents® novels. These books have a cover price of $3.99 each in the U.S. and $4.50 each in Canada, but they are yours to keep absolutely free.
3. There's no catch! You're under no obligation to buy anything. We charge nothing—ZERO—for your first shipment. And you don't have to make any minimum number of purchases—not even one!
4. The fact is thousands of readers enjoy receiving their books by mail from the Harlequin Reader Service®. They enjoy the convenience of home delivery...they like getting the best new novels at discount prices, BEFORE they're available in stores...and they love their *Heart to Heart* subscriber newsletter featuring author news, horoscopes, recipes, book reviews and much more!
5. We hope that after receiving your free books you'll want to remain a subscriber. But the choice is yours—to continue or cancel, any time at all! So why not take us up on our invitation, with no risk of any kind. You'll be glad you did!

Visit us online at

www.eHarlequin.com

- ◆ **Exciting Harlequin® romance novels—FREE!**
- ◆ **Plus an exciting mystery gift—FREE!**
- ◆ **No cost! No obligation to buy!**

The Harlequin Reader Service®—Here's how it works:

Accepting your 2 free books and gift places you under no obligation to buy anything. You may keep the books and gift and return the shipping statement marked "cancel." If you do not cancel, about a month later we'll send you 6 additional novels and bill you just $3.34 each in the U.S., or $3.74 each in Canada, plus 25¢ shipping & handling per book and applicable taxes if any.* That's the complete price and — compared to cover prices of $3.99 each in the U.S. and $4.50 each in Canada — it's quite a bargain! You may cancel at any time, but if you choose to continue, every month we'll send you 6 more books, which you may either purchase at the discount price or return to us and cancel your subscription.

*Terms and prices subject to change without notice. Sales tax applicable in N.Y. Canadian residents will be charged applicable provincial taxes and GST.

If offer card is missing write to: Harlequin Reader Service, 3010 Walden Ave., P.O. Box 1867, Buffalo, NY 14240-1867 fiancée was the only reason you wanted to leave, and you haven't yet answered.'

'It's the main one,' she replied, with some truth.

'What other reasons are there? Or perhaps you can't think of any offhand?'

In desperation, she stammered, 'Kirk w-wouldn't want me to be here if he knew that...'

'That we'd once been lovers? And almost were again?'

'He'd be furious.'

'If he could abandon you here, as he appears to have done, I doubt if he'd care a damn,' Blaze disagreed coolly.

Giving up all pretence, she pleaded, 'Surely the fact that I *want* to go is enough?'

'I'm afraid not. It's what *I* want that counts.'

'I don't understand why you want me to stay,' she told him helplessly.

Heavy lids drooping, he glanced at her through his lashes. 'Perhaps I regret last night... Regret not having taken advantage of your...shall we say susceptibility?'

Her heart lurched, but, knowing he was just taunting her, she said hardily, 'I can assure you I've no intention of behaving so stupidly a second time. And as your fiancée will be here...'

'I'm beginning to seriously doubt it.'

'Well, whether she comes or not—'

But he was shaking his head, his face adamant. 'I'm afraid there are far too many unanswered questions for me to allow you to leave just yet...'

Shocking in its suddenness, the phone shrilled, making Fran jump.

'Ah!' Blaze murmured softly. 'With a bit of luck this may help to answer some of them.'

CHAPTER SIX

'IF YOU'LL excuse me?' He rose to his feet and reached for the receiver. 'Balantyne. Good... Yes... I see... When...?'

Listening intently to what Blaze was saying, and watching his dark, intent face, Fran held her breath, but neither his words nor his expression gave anything away.

'Yes... Yes, do that... Thanks for letting me know.'

Replacing the receiver, he stood, his well-shaped head a little bent, gazing into space.

Her eyes fixed on him, she waited.

When after perhaps a minute he was still silent, unable to bear the tension a moment longer, she asked, 'It wasn't...?'

He lifted his head to look at her. His face was cool and shuttered. 'No, it wasn't Melinda. However, the call did provide a clue as to her whereabouts.'

Resuming his seat, he went on, his voice dispassionate, 'With the pair of them being missing, I'd begun to wonder if she and Varley might have run off together—'

'I would doubt it,' Fran broke in drily.

Blaze gave her a wry glance. 'Either you're very sure of him, or you don't think Melinda is the type to sacrifice a wealthy husband for a fling with a man—however handsome and charming—on the verge of bankruptcy... Which is it?

'No, don't bother to tell me; I can see by your face. You're not at all sure of Varley—'

'Whereas you're *quite* sure of Miss Ross.'

It wasn't in Fran's nature to be catty, and as soon as the

words were out she regretted them. 'I'm sorry. I had no right to say that.' Then, awkwardly, 'Please go on.'

'The call was from the detective agency...' Seeing the expression on Fran's face, he shook his head. 'There's no need to look so horrified. You can't seriously believe I was having Melinda watched?'

'I wouldn't put anything past you.'

Caught on the raw, a white line appeared round his mouth, and, watching him fight for control, Fran wished the words unsaid.

After a moment, the battle won, he visibly relaxed, and she gave a sigh of relief.

'Perhaps I asked for that,' he said levelly. 'But the other precautions I took have proved to be necessary.'

'I can't see that they have,' she disagreed boldly. Then, her resentment obvious, 'It wasn't necessary to have either myself or Kirk watched. I know things haven't gone quite according to plan, but in the main everything has worked out—'

'Before you go any further,' Blaze broke in coldly, 'perhaps you'd better wait and hear what I have to say.'

With a sudden feeling of apprehension, she closed her mouth and waited.

'After shaking off his shadow, Varley did a neat disappearing trick. Though a couple of the men from the agency cast around they were unable to pick up his trail. But it seems he got a bit too confident, and he made the mistake of going back to his apartment, which was still being watched.

'Perhaps his plans had changed, or maybe he'd gone to pick up something important he'd forgotten... But, whatever, he only stayed a short time. The really intriguing thing is this: *he wasn't alone...*'

As the implications sank in, Fran's eyes widened.

'The woman who was with him was described as a good-looking blonde, about five foot six and slimly built, driving a white Porsche.'

'It doesn't make sense,' Fran whispered dazedly.

'That's what I thought at first,' Blaze agreed grimly. 'But I'm rapidly changing my mind. If one thing I already suspect is true, it makes a great deal of sense. But until I have confirmation...'

A knock at the door cut through his words.

'Come in.'

The door opened to admit the butler, who, having cleared his throat, said verbosely, 'I'm sorry to disturb you, sir, but you gave instructions that you were to be told as soon as Mr Henderson arrived.'

'He's here?'

'Yes, sir. Hannah has just shown him into the main living room.'

'Thank you, Mortimer. Please tell Mr Henderson I'll be down directly.'

As the door closed behind the stately black-clad figure Blaze turned to Fran, and, a glint in his eye she was unable to decipher, suggested, 'Perhaps you'd like to come with me? You may find it interesting.'

Something about the invitation and the way he was watching her made all her nerves start to jangle.

'Very well.' Taking a deep breath, and doing her best to appear calm and composed, though her legs were oddly shaky, she accompanied him down the stairs, one hand on the banister.

They had reached the main hall, which had been transformed for the party, when he stopped and said, 'Oh, just one thing. I'd prefer it if you didn't wear this.' Before she could guess his intention he had removed Kirk's ring and slipped it into his pocket.

When they reached the living room, a stocky man in his

late fifties, with grizzled hair and twinkling hazel eyes, rose to his feet. He was wearing well-cut evening clothes.

'Edward. Long time no see... I got your message.' He held out his hand.

'Richard.' The two men shook hands cordially. 'I hope my asking you to come early didn't inconvenience you too much?'

'Not at all. Since Edna died I've only had myself to consider. And, as you know, I'm always glad to be of service.'

Blaze put an arm around Fran's slender waist and drew her forward. 'Darling, may I introduce you to Richard Henderson, an old friend of the family? Richard, I'd like you to meet Francesca Holt.'

Thrown by the *darling*, she stammered, 'H-how do you do, Mr Henderson.'

'Richard, please, and I hope I may call you Francesca?'

'Of course.' A pleasant, open face, and a slight gap between his two front teeth gave him a boyish look, and, taking an instant liking to him, she answered his friendly smile.

He enfolded her hand in a light but firm grip. 'It's very nice to meet you. I was delighted when Edward mentioned that it was to be an engagement party. In my humble opinion he's been a bachelor for far too long.'

'Oh, but I'm not—'

'Richard is a highly respected QC,' Blaze broke in smoothly, 'but his other great interest—one in which he's an acknowledged expert—is jewellery and precious stones.'

Turning to the older man, he said, 'Like everyone else, you're here to enjoy yourself, but before the other guests arrive I was hoping you would take a look at Francesca's necklace and tell me what you think.'

'So that's why you suggested I brought my glass,'

Richard said cheerfully. 'Well, I'm more than happy to sing for my supper.'

Since *jewellery and precious stones* had been mentioned Blaze had been watching Fran's face for any sign of discomfort, but the only emotion he could find there was a look of perplexity.

'Why don't you sit down?' He steered her to a chair.

Instead of going to the safe, as she'd expected, Blaze drew the leather pouch from his pocket and handed it to the other man. Surprised, she wondered why he'd been carrying so valuable a thing around with him.

Opening the drawstring, Richard tipped out the glittering contents, 'The Balantyne rubies, of course!' he exclaimed. 'I remember the last time I saw these was at your mother and father's wedding...' Then, sounding puzzled, 'There's the same number of stones, but they look entirely different.'

'We've just had them reset.'

'A great improvement, if I may say so. The new design shows the stones off to much better advantage.'

'I thought so too,' Blaze agreed.

'So you'd like my opinion?'

At Blaze's nod, Richard fitted a jeweller's glass into his eye and gave the necklace a long and careful examination. Then, putting it back in the pouch, he handed it to Blaze and returned the glass to his pocket.

'Well, I must congratulate you. The actual workmanship is very fine, and though the stones themselves wouldn't stand up to expert scrutiny, it's really an excellent fake. With today's technological advances it looks, to all intents and purposes, as good as the real thing, and would fool most people.

'As far as I'm concerned it makes a lot of sense for your future wife to wear this, and keep the original safe in the bank vaults.'

'Thanks. That's more or less what I expected you to say.'

Clapping him on the shoulder. Blaze added, 'Now, if you don't mind, it's high time Francesca and I went to get ready for this party... I don't need to tell you to ring for anything you want, and to make yourself at home.'

Turning to Fran, who was sitting in stunned silence, he urged her to her feet. 'Come on, darling, we need to change into our glad rags.'

Limp and unresisting, like someone in a state of shock, she allowed herself to be shepherded from the room.

When they reached Blaze's private sitting room he tossed the pouch carelessly on to the coffee table; the drawstring hadn't been tightened, and a length of the necklace spilled from it.

The storm had finally moved away, and a ray of watery sun slanting through the window picked out the rubies like a spotlight.

Staring at it as though hypnotised, Fran denied hoarsely, 'It can't be a fake! It *can't*! There must be some mistake.'

'Oh, there's been a mistake all right,' Blaze agreed grimly. 'And Varley made it. But we haven't time to discuss it now. The other guests will be arriving before too long.'

Her jaw dropped. 'You're not going ahead with the party?'

'It's much too late to cancel it.'

'But how will you...?'

'Explain Melinda's absence? I won't. I have no intention of looking a complete fool by having to admit that another man has stolen not only the Balantyne rubies, but my fiancée along with them.'

'B-but I thought the whole point was to introduce Miss Ross to—'

'The whole point was to introduce my *fiancée*... It's fortunate that none of the people coming here tonight have met Melinda...or even know her name, for that matter...'

After a brief, but significant pause, he went on blandly, 'So it should be relatively easy to find a substitute fiancée—'

Light beginning to dawn, Fran broke in, 'You don't mean that you want *me* to...?'

'That's exactly what I mean. It's the only answer. I'd already decided that before we went downstairs.'

'So that's why you called me *darling*,' she said in a strangled voice. 'Why you acted as you did. You wanted Mr Henderson to believe...'

'That you were my intended,' he finished for her drily. 'And he did. Richard is one of the shrewdest men I know, and he never gave it a second thought, so we should have no trouble convincing the rest.'

If Blaze had meant nothing to her she might have been able to carry it off. But, feeling as she did, she couldn't bear to pretend. Couldn't bear to stand by his side and receive all the good wishes intended for another woman. It would break her heart.

'No,' she protested raggedly. 'I won't do it.'

'My dear Francesca, you have no option. You're in this right up to your beautiful neck.'

'But I'm not! I hadn't the faintest idea there was anything going on between Kirk and Melinda. And if the necklace *is* a fake I swear I didn't know.'

'I only have your word for that. *You* were the one who delivered it... So unless you want to end up in prison, along with your ex-boyfriend, you'll do exactly as I say.'

'No,' she cried in a panic. 'I won't let you coerce me. I haven't done anything wrong—'

'Even supposing that's true, it won't be easy to prove it.'

'It *is* true!'

He shrugged. 'It hardly matters whether it is or not. When Varleys folds, as it's bound to, you'll need another post. Once it gets into the papers that their up-and-coming designer has been mixed up in something like this...'

Watching her face, seeing the look of despair that his words evoked, he said, 'Exactly. Even if you're whiter than white, mud has a nasty habit of sticking. You'll be finished in the jewellery business.'

Still she made an effort to fight back. 'I'll find another career. I've done it before.'

'But you won't do it again. I'll make sure of that.'

'Then I'll take a job as a shop assistant, or a waitress.'

Shaking his head, he said with deadly intent, 'If you refuse to do as I ask, I'll see that you don't get a job of any kind. And should you manage to *get* one, even if it's stacking shelves in a supermarket, I'll make certain you don't keep it.'

Appalled, she whispered, 'You can't hound me like that!'

He laughed, white teeth gleaming. 'I assure you I can! I can wield quite a lot of power, direct or indirect, when I choose to.'

Bitterly, she said, 'I'm surprised you think I'm worth the trouble.'

'My motto has always been *Don't get mad, get even*. I don't allow anyone to make a fool of me and walk away unscathed.'

'But I had nothing to do with it.'

'You may not have helped *plan* the whole thing, in fact I'm sure you didn't, but you certainly played your part. Even if it was unwittingly, you came here and stalled me long enough to give Varley a chance to get a head start. Now we've reached the end of the line. You owe me, Francesca, and you'll do what I want you to do.

'How much conviction you put into the part is, of course, up to you. But, unless you want to answer to me afterwards, I suggest that you try to make it look credible. At least while other people are present... And, speaking of other people, our guests are due to arrive in something like three-quarters of an hour, so suppose you start to get ready?'

Resenting his arrogant assumption that she would knuckle under, she told him coldly, 'I've nothing grand enough to wear. All I brought was a simple cocktail dress.'

'Wear that,' he ordered briefly. Then, with a frown, 'What colour is it?'

'Black.' As she spoke she remembered with malicious satisfaction that he disliked black.

Judging by the gleam in his eye he read her mind, but all he said was, 'Black will do fine.'

'I'm afraid that when I decided to leave here I packed in a hurry, so it's bound to be badly creased.'

'Then wear something of Melinda's. You're about the same size, and at least she had good taste. There's a wardrobe full of dresses, most of which she's never had on.'

Chin up, Fran faced him defiantly. 'I wouldn't dream of wearing another woman's clothes!'

His white teeth snapped together. Stepping forward, he took her chin in his hand and, splayed fingers and thumb biting in a little, lifted her face to his. 'If you're not ready in thirty minutes,' he warned her softly, 'I'll come and dress you myself.'

Releasing her abruptly, he turned and walked away.

Trembling in every limb, she watched his broad back disappear into his bedroom. If he'd flown into a rage and shouted she could have defied him more easily, but she'd found his quiet, leashed anger intimidating.

And she wasn't the only one to find it so.

In the business world, she recalled, he was noted as a man who was always in control, a man who never raised his voice, yet he was both feared and respected, not only by his staff but by his equals.

Making an effort, she pulled herself together. The seconds were flying past, and if she wasn't ready in time she didn't doubt that he was quite capable of carrying out his threat.

Biting her lip, she went into Melinda's bedroom and opened the case she'd left there.

As she had surmised, the black dress was unwearable, and now it was too late she found herself wishing that she'd packed with greater care instead of just bundling everything in.

With the utmost reluctance she went over to the wardrobe and looked at the row of evening dresses with the rack of matching shoes.

There wasn't a single black amongst them, she noted. Most were strong, vibrant colours...blue...green...scarlet... Closer inspection showed that many of them had no back and very little front, and several were lacy and see-through.

Perhaps as a result of her upbringing, and her dislike of drawing attention to herself, Fran had always tended to dress down, avoiding bright colours and the more daring styles.

With the best will in the world, she couldn't see herself in any of these striking creations.

Right at the end, pushed carelessly to one side, as though Melinda had regretted her choice, was an ankle-length smoke-grey chiffon.

Relatively modest and perfectly plain, with plaited straps which continued beneath the bust-line, it appeared to be exactly her size. A piece of tissue paper lining the bodice confirmed the fact that it had never been worn.

The matching shoes, Fran noted, were a size too large. But her own grey evening shoes would go with it perfectly. Her mind made up, she hurriedly lifted it out, removed the tissue paper, and laid it across the bed.

She found herself hoping very much that Blaze would approve her choice.

Within the last few minutes her resentment at his high-handedness had died. A deep-rooted honesty made her admit that his anger was justified.

If the necklace *was* a fake—and though it was hard to believe it seemed unlikely that Richard Henderson could have made a mistake—Blaze had been robbed of a priceless family heirloom as well as the woman he was all set to marry.

She recalled his haughty statement, *'I've learnt to keep what's mine while I want it,'* and shivered. All his carefully laid plans had been ruined, and he'd been left in the kind of situation that could make any man look a fool.

In the circumstances, she couldn't blame him for venting his anger and frustration on her. Nothing was solely black and white, and though what had happened wasn't her fault, she had been involved, and felt at least partly responsible.

But it was too late to change anything. The only thing she could possibly do was try to make amends. So if she was forced to go through with this heartbreaking charade then for both their sakes she would endeavour to look her best, and play the part as well as she could.

After a quick shower to freshen herself up, she put on her prettiest undies and her finest silk stockings, before coiling her hair into a shining knot and making up with care.

When she was ready, she slipped into the cloud of chiffon and pulled up the concealed zip. Two things immediately became clear. The dress fitted exactly, and it was nowhere near as demure as she'd first thought.

Stepping in front of the cheval-glass, she gasped at the vision that stared back at her. She had never looked like this in her life before.

The bust section was cunningly cut to reveal the enticing swell of her breasts and the valley between, and as she moved the floating layers of gauzy material parted to disclose that, on the left, the skirt was slit up to the thigh.

Fran was still standing bemused when there was a peremptory rap and the door opened.

Blaze's reflection appeared in the mirror behind her. Freshly shaven, his hair parted on the left and smoothly brushed, he looked extremely handsome in immaculate evening dress.

For a long moment he stood perfectly still. Then he turned her around and stood gazing down at her, a look on his face that made her stammered 'W-will I do?' superfluous.

'You look stunning,' he said softly. 'A million dollars and then some... And the colour is perfect with this.' As he spoke he produced the necklace.

She glanced at it with a sudden distaste.

Reading her expression, he said, 'Everyone who knows the Balantyne family history will be expecting my fiancée to be wearing it. And, let's face it, you've worn it before, so I can't see any problem... Unless you object to wearing something that's been confirmed as a fake?'

She shook her head. 'It's not that... I—I just feel...' Unable to put into words exactly how she did feel, she made a gesture of submission and reached for the necklace.

'Stand still; I'll fasten it for you.' While she stood obediently, he put it around her slim throat, secured the clasp, and settled it into place.

Stepping back to admire the effect, he commented laconically, 'For a fake it looks well enough...'

A glance in the mirror confirmed that his words were an understatement.

'It's a pity we haven't got the real thing for you to wear,' he went on, 'though I strongly suspect that rubies aren't your stones. You need the more subtle gems, like opals and moonstones... Speaking of which...'

He drew a small leather ring box from his pocket and

took out an unusual and very lovely half-hoop of pearly moonstones.

'An engagement party calls for an engagement ring. This was my paternal grandmother's. I think it's your size.'

Lifting Fran's left hand, he slipped it on to her third finger. It fitted perfectly, and went with the ensemble as though it had all been minutely planned. Blaze nodded. 'Ideal, I think.'

It was one of the loveliest rings Fran had ever seen, and, suddenly close to tears, she thought, *If only this was for real.*

But of course it wasn't. It was as fake as the necklace. A charade to be played out to save Blaze embarrassment in front of his friends and colleagues. When they discovered that the actual wedding was off, he would no doubt say that the engagement had been ended 'by mutual consent' or whatever excuse would cause the least speculation...

Watching her face, he lifted a dark brow. 'You don't like it?'

'Yes, I do,' she contradicted huskily. 'It's absolutely beautiful.'

'Then why look so unhappy?'

Before she could think of an answer, he said half angrily, 'I'm sorry. I'm a stupid, insensitive oaf. Of course you're unhappy. Varley may have run off with my fiancée, but Melinda's run off with yours. And at the moment you probably consider your loss is greater than mine. I was simply buying myself a suitable wife, whereas you loved Varley.'

Not knowing what to say, and very conscious of his nearness, she finally stammered, 'Shouldn't we be going down? I—I mean your guests will be arriving any minute.'

'*Our* guests,' he corrected her. 'And of course you're quite right... But I think we should make time for one more thing.'

Before she could ask what that was, he drew her into his arms, said half mockingly, 'It's just as well you don't wear lipstick,' and kissed her.

Unable to help herself, her lips parted to the seductive demand of his, and with no thought of charades or pretence she melted against him while he kissed her as though she was the only woman he had ever wanted.

After a long moment he lifted his head and smiled into her eyes. 'That's much better,' he said with undisguised satisfaction. 'Now you look all flushed and glowing, exactly like a bride-to-be who's just been thoroughly kissed.'

Was that why he'd kissed her? she wondered. So that she wouldn't appear sad and wan in front of his friends and colleagues?

Stroking a fingertip down her warm cheek, he queried, 'Ready to run the gauntlet?'

As ready as she would ever be, she nodded.

Blaze's arm around her waist, they descended the stairs just as Richard Henderson appeared in the hall.

He came over, and, catching sight of the bruises on her arm, asked jokingly, 'Has Edward been beating you already?'

Shaking her head with a smile, she said, 'A slight accident on the way here. I would have worn a long-sleeved dress had it been possible.'

'Speaking for myself, I'm rather pleased it wasn't.' Eyeing the grey chiffon appreciatively, he added, 'Just the sight of you makes me feel young again.'

'You don't think it's too daring?' she asked.

'I certainly don't. You look absolutely wonderful! Now, I'd better not detain you...I see there are more guests arriving.'

Amongst the first was Lady Melford, a sharp-eyed, frankly-spoken dowager, who described herself as, 'A near neighbour, and one of the family's oldest friends.'

The introductions over, that redoubtable lady enquired of Fran, 'So how long have you and Edward known each other, my dear?'

Uncertain what to say, Fran hesitated, and looked at Blaze for guidance.

'For about three years,' he replied smoothly, and with perfect truth.

'Then why have you kept it a secret all this time?'

Tongue-in-cheek, he answered, 'It's only quite recently that Francesca gave in to my...er...demands, and consented to become my fiancée.'

Turning to Fran, Lady Melford commented, 'Very sensible, my dear. I strongly disapprove of these modern young females who are willing to jump into bed with a man after only a few hours' acquaintance.'

His grey eyes ironic, Blaze glanced at Fran before replying gravely, 'Francesca would never have done a thing like that, would you, darling?'

Itching to kick him hard, she felt her cheeks growing hot.

Taking note of the younger woman's heightening colour, Lady Melford said, 'Forgive me, my dear, if my plain speaking has embarrassed you.'

Fran shook her head in a smiling if somewhat flustered disclaimer. 'Of course it hasn't.'

'You've chosen well, Edward.' Lady Melford gave her verdict. 'So many young men these days end up with a wife as hard as nails and "worldly"—whatever that means. It's most refreshing to meet a bride-to-be who is obviously in love and still capable of blushing... I'm sure you'll both be very happy...

'Now, I see Richard is already here. I must go and say hello to him while you greet some more of your guests...'

Fran breathed an inward sigh of relief as the impressive

silver-haired dowager left them to bear down purposefully on Richard Henderson.

Bending his dark head, Blaze murmured in Fran's ear, 'You've passed with flying colours. It isn't easy to earn Lady Melford's approval... Ah, here's Sir Humphrey Waldon, and his wife Judith...I think you'll like them...'

'I'm sure I will,' she assured him steadily.

Throughout the long evening, while an excellent buffet was served and the champagne flowed freely, they circulated amongst groups of people who were clearly having fun and enjoying the party.

Apart from a moment or two, when he crossed the hall to have a quick word with Mortimer, who was keeping an eagle eye on things, Blaze never left her side.

Pleasantly fielding any awkward questions, he gave a good impression of a relaxed and carefree host, with no concerns apart from showing off his fiancée, and the comfort of his guests.

For her part, making perhaps the biggest effort of her life, Fran talked and smiled, and received all the good wishes with grace and charm.

Though she felt as if she was being flayed, no one would have guessed she wasn't the radiant bride-to-be that she appeared.

Once in a while, in his role of prospective bridegroom, Blaze would smile into her eyes and give her hand a squeeze.

Though she knew quite well it was only play-acting, each time her heart seemed to turn right over.

Maybe because of the strain she was under, and the need to keep smiling when she felt more like weeping, the evening dragged endlessly.

By the time twelve o'clock came she was exhausted, and to add to her discomfort her ankle had begun to protest at the high heels she wore.

But, a smile pinned to her lips, she stood by Blaze's side until the very last couple were ready to make their farewells. Then, shivering a little in the cool night air, she helped to wave them off.

As soon as the chauffeur-driven car had drawn away, he urged her inside and closed the door. Stepping awkwardly on her throbbing ankle, she winced.

'Ankle hurting?' he asked.

'A bit,' she confessed.

As she spoke, Mortimer and a couple of the servants appeared, to deal with the debris of the party.

Blaze waved them away. 'For heaven's sake, man, it'll keep until morning. The entire household has had a long day. I suggest you just lock up and get off to bed.'

'Thank you, sir.' The butler cleared his throat, and then, his manner as impeccable as his clothes, went on, 'May I, on behalf of myself and the other members of the staff, respectfully tender congratulations and all good wishes for you and your fiancée's future happiness.'

'Thank you, Mortimer.'

Inclining his head, the butler added, 'The fire in your sitting room has been replenished, and a Thermos flask of hot chocolate taken up. Will there be anything else, sir?'

'No, nothing, thanks. Goodnight, Mortimer.'

The butler gave a little bow. 'Goodnight, sir. Goodnight, miss.'

'Goodnight, Mortimer.'

Throughout, the manservant's face and manner had remained impassive, but for the first time it occurred to Fran to wonder what he and the rest of the staff thought of the sudden change in fiancée.

As the black-coated figure moved away, once again reading her mind, Blaze remarked *sotto voce*, 'I doubt if anything surprises Mortimer... And if it did he certainly wouldn't show it...'

Then, before she could even begin to guess his intention, he stooped, and, picking her up in his arms, headed for the stairs. 'We'd better save that ankle. You'll want to be able to walk on it tomorrow.'

CHAPTER SEVEN

Remembering only too clearly what had happened the previous night, when it was too late to remember, replied put the house in trouble.

Feeling the involuntary movement, he queried, 'Cold?'

'No.' Even his voice shook.

He glanced down at her, 'No,' with a knowing smile 'I don't tell you to the heart. You're afraid of a repeat of last night.'

For the spasm answer enough.

'Well, you don't need to worry.' He wanted her quietly enough have absolutely, 'no intention of letting the same thing happen again.'

She relaxed slightly. If he meant to turn put her away, the arms of her bedroom and walk away there, would be nothing to worry about.

When they reached the top of the stairs, however, instead of turning towards her room he headed for the long gallery.

'Where are you taking me?'

Back to my suite.

Alarmed about, she asked, 'Why?'

'Didn't you say Katrina say there would be a use the one's flask of hot chocolate waiting?'

Part had remember that the butler had arranged to bring him into a bracket. But, suddenly recalling what there had said about no one venturing up to the suite without express instructions, she realised, but she had been glad.

'The voice during,' she said. 'You gave answer.'

'He made me attempt to do this. I've one thing seeming had very little need forget. For another, I thought we took

Then, before she could even begin to expel his intrusion,
he stooped and, picking her up in his arms, headed for the
stairs. 'We'll soon have that ankle. You'll want to be able
to walk on it tomorrow...'

CHAPTER SEVEN

REMEMBERING only too clearly what had happened the previous night, Fran felt every nerve in her body tighten and
she began to tremble.

Feeling the involuntary movement, he queried, 'Cold?'

'No.' Even her voice shook.

He glanced down at her. 'So what's bothering you? No,
don't tell me, let me guess. You're afraid of a repeat of last
night?'

Her silence was answer enough.

'Well, you don't need to worry,' he assured her quizzically. 'I have absolutely no intention of letting the same
thing happen again.'

She relaxed slightly. If he meant to just put her down at
the door of her bedroom and walk away there would be
nothing to worry about.

When they reached the top of the stairs, however, instead
of turning towards her room he headed for the long gallery.

'Where are you taking me?'

'Back to my suite.'

Alarmed afresh, she asked, 'Why?'

'Didn't you hear Mortimer say there would be a nice fire
and a flask of hot chocolate waiting?'

Fran had presumed that the butler had arranged both for
his master's benefit. But, suddenly recalling what Blaze had
said about no one venturing up to his suite without express
instructions, she realised that this had been planned.

Her tone accusing, she said, 'You gave orders...'

He made no attempt to deny it. 'For one thing, you've
had very little to eat tonight. For another, I thought we both

needed to unwind for ten minutes or so before going to bed.'

'Oh, but I—'

'And, if you remember, you left your case up there.'

It all sounded very logical, yet some sixth sense screamed danger. If he once kissed her, touched her, as he had the previous night—

Snapping off the thought, she reminded herself a shade desperately of Blaze's mocking assurance. *'I have absolutely no intention of letting the same thing happen again.'*

When they reached his suite the plum-coloured velvet curtains had been drawn over the windows and the room looked cosy and welcoming, with its diffused lighting and glowing fire.

Shouldering the door closed, Blaze put her down on the settee, her back propped against some cushions, and slipped off her shoes.

When she would have swung her legs to the floor, he said crisply, 'Better keep that foot up if you don't want it to swell.'

The possibility made her hesitate. She wanted to be able to leave tomorrow.

If Blaze would let her...

But now she had finished playing the role of fiancée, and he'd admitted that he no longer suspected her of being a prime mover in the plot, surely there would be no reason to make her stay?

'Ready for some hot chocolate?' he asked.

'Please.'

He took the top off the Thermos jug and poured the creamy liquid into two mugs. Passing her one, he instructed, 'Careful, it's quite hot.'

Holding it in both hands, she took a sip. It was deliciously light, yet satisfying. 'Mmm...that's good,' she murmured.

Picking up his own mug, Blaze sat down on the settee by her legs.

In response to her involuntary shift away, he queried blandly, 'Not crowding you, I hope?'

Disturbed by the movement, the material of her skirt parted company.

Before Fran could reach to pull it into place Blaze half turned and, after admiring the expanse of slender silk-clad leg and thigh, with his free hand he carefully rearranged the grey chiffon.

'Thank you,' she said in a strangled voice.

He leered at her theatrically. 'Always willing to be of service.'

All at once, in response to the laughter in his eyes, a smile tugged at her lips.

'That's better,' he applauded. 'I was afraid you'd lost your sense of humour.'

'I haven't had much to laugh about lately.'

'No, the last couple of days can't have been a lot of fun.'

That was the understatement of the year, Fran thought as she sipped. Fate had dealt her so many blows that she was starting to feel well and truly battered...

All at once, whether from lack of concentration or sheer weariness, the mug in her hand tilted, spilling the remaining hot chocolate down the front of her dress and into her lap.

She gave a cry of horror.

Jumping up, Blaze demanded urgently, 'Are you scalded?'

'No. No. But the *dress*...!'

As he took the empty mug from her hand and put it on the tray beside his own, she stumbled to her feet and headed for Melinda's room.

'Don't worry about the dress.'

Ignoring his injunction, she unzipped it and stepped out

of it as quickly as possible. Then hurrying through to the bathroom, she began to sponge away the worst of the mess.

How *could* someone who was usually quite careful have been so downright clumsy? she chided herself.

It wouldn't have mattered a jot if it had been off the peg and her own, but this was an expensive designer model belonging to another woman...

When she'd got the dress as clean as possible, she hung it on a hanger and briefly considered what to do next.

The chocolate had soaked through to her skin, and her delicate undies were stained and sticky.

After a moment's thought, she decided that as her case was here the most sensible thing would be to shower at once, clean her teeth, and put on her night things. That way, as soon as she reached her own room she could drop straight into bed.

A glance in the mirror reminded her that she was still wearing the necklace. Taking it off, she put both that and Blaze's ring carefully on the dressing table, before returning to the bathroom to strip off her undies and step into the shower.

Some five minutes later, her hair loose about her shoulders and still slightly damp, she donned an ivory satin nightdress and a robe, which she belted securely. Then, putting all her things into her case, she zipped it up and, that in one hand and the necklace and ring in the other, returned to the living room.

Blaze, who was standing with his back to the fire, came over. 'You've only just made it. Another thirty seconds and I was coming in to get you.' Eyeing the case, he queried, 'Going somewhere?'

Ignoring the levity, she handed him the necklace and the ring and said, 'I've done what I could with the dress...'

He slipped the ring into his pocket, tossed the necklace carelessly on to the bureau and, taking the case from her hand, set it down by the wall, before leading her back to the fire.

Without knowing quite how she got there, Fran found herself stretched out on the settee once more, with Blaze by her side.

Anxiously, she added, 'I only hope it's not ruined.'

'The dress isn't important,' he said firmly, 'apart from the fact that you looked so sensational wearing it.'

As her cheeks flushed with pleasure, he went on seriously, 'I was proud of you tonight. You played the part of fiancée beautifully... Which reminds me...'

Taking the ring from his pocket, he slipped it back on to her finger and touched his lips to it.

'Moonstones, like opals, should be worn all the time, even in bed. See how these glow? They pine and grow dull if they're put away, or the wrong person wears them.'

His romantic words and action made her heart melt, even while a sense of self preservation warned that such a feeling was dangerous.

Watching her face, he said softly, 'And speaking of bed, it's about time you went. It's been a tiring evening and you're looking shattered.'

'I didn't sleep very well last night,' she confessed.

He surprised her by saying, 'Neither did I. But hopefully we can remedy that tonight.' Then, with a lift of one brow, 'You don't look very optimistic?'

She wasn't. Though she was weary, with such a lot on her mind she didn't see how she could possibly sleep.

Helplessly, she said, 'There's so much unresolved...so many things there's been no time to even think about, let alone discuss. Suppose we were wrong in presuming Melinda and Kirk had run off together? There might be some other explanation.'

'I very much doubt it.'

'And if the necklace really *is* a fake—'

'There's nothing can be done at the moment,' he broke in decidedly. 'So I can't see any point in staying awake and worrying.'

'I don't think I can help it,' she admitted.

Leaning towards her, his eyes fixed on her mouth, he said with soft intent, 'Well, I'm sure I can take your mind off things.'

Too late she realised the danger. 'No! Please, Blaze, don't...'

But his hands cupped her face, lifting it to his, and that hovering mouth swooped and claimed hers.

His kiss was light, almost experimental, searching for a response that, lips pressed together, she fought hard to withhold. The tip of his tongue brushed over them, coaxing them to part, finding the soft, sensitive inner skin, making her shudder.

One hand slid beneath her tumbled hair, finding the warmth of her nape, while the other moved to caress the curve of her breast.

Already her eager body was longing for his touch, and in just a moment or two her need would swamp her common sense and then she would be lost...

Somehow she tore her mouth free and gasped, 'You said you had no intention of kissing me.'

'I said I had no intention of letting the same thing happen tonight that happened last night.'

'But this *is* what happened last night.'

'No, it isn't. Last night we both slept alone...or rather *didn't* sleep. A cold shower had little effect. And I don't plan to take another one. Tonight I intend to have a hot shower and go to bed with my fiancée.'

In a panic, she cried, 'No! I've done as you asked so far. I've taken Melinda's place at the party. But I've no intention of taking her place in your bed. I *won't* be a substitute—'

'Who said anything about a substitute?' he broke in coldly. 'In any case, you'll be anything I want you to be. As I pointed out earlier this evening, you owe me...'

'Don't force me to sleep with you,' she begged.

'You know as well as I do that there won't be any need for force. Sexually we've always struck sparks off each other. Last night, when we were both committed, you would have let it happen. You *wanted* it to happen. Tonight we're both free, so what's the problem?'

The problem was that, loving him as she did, she couldn't bear to just feel *used*... At the very least she wanted him to want *her*...

But she could hardly tell him that.

Jerkily, she said, 'I've never gone in for one-night stands or short-term affairs—'

'You did once,' he reminded her cruelly.

'And one mistake was enough.'

The dark face hardened. 'So you regard it as a mistake?'

'What else can I regard it as?'

'I see,' he said silkily. 'And you don't want to make the same mistake twice? Well, that's too bad...'

He got to his feet, and in one swift movement stooped and lifted her high in his arms.

'I'll just have to see that it's a mistake you enjoy making...'

His bedroom had plain white walls and black polished oak floorboards. It was simply furnished, apart from a magnificent four-poster with a crimson and gold canopy.

He put her down on the bed and went to turn the key in the lock.

'What are you doing?' she gasped.

'Making sure you don't run away while I take a shower.'

'I hate the idea of being locked in,' she protested hoarsely.

'In that case you have two choices. Either you come in the bathroom with me...'

'I certainly will not.'

'Or you give me your word to stay put.'

When she bit her lip and remained silent, he said, 'Just as I thought.' Taking the key, he dropped it into his pocket, promising, 'I won't keep you waiting long.'

Fran watched the bathroom door close behind him with a tumult of mixed feelings...fear and longing, anger and anticipation...

Her mind, her will, still fought against being coerced in this way, while adrenalin pumped through her veins, fuelling a growing excitement.

She couldn't deny that she yearned for him. But she knew that while tonight his lovemaking would be sweeter than wine, tomorrow, the knowledge that she'd been merely a substitute for Melinda would be as bitter as Dead Sea apples.

However, if he was determined to take her, she would have little choice in the matter. He wouldn't make any attempt to force her; she was certain of that. But then, as he'd already pointed out, he wouldn't need to.

Her body was more his than her own, and though her mind and her will would put up a token resistance, they would soon be overwhelmed and vanquished...

The bathroom door opening brought her bolt upright.

As Blaze strolled in she felt her heart lurch. She'd seen him naked before, but she had almost forgotten how beautiful he was.

'Beautiful' seemed a very feminine way to describe so masculine a man. But one dictionary definition of the word was, *'delighting the aesthetic senses'*, so it was apt.

He had both strength and symmetry, with wide shoulders, narrow hips, long, straight legs and an elegant line to his spine.

His smooth, healthy skin gleamed like oiled silk, while a scattering of crisp body hair pooled on his chest and vee'd down to his flat stomach.

Though a tall, powerful man, he moved lithely, with an almost feline grace, and Fran held her breath as she watched him cross the room.

He came and sat on the edge of the bed. His dark hair was slightly rumpled, a single lock falling over his forehead, and in spite of their brilliance his grey eyes appeared almost black.

'I'd prefer it if you didn't look as though you were afraid of me,' he said abruptly. 'I know you want this as much as I do.'

'One part of me does,' she admitted. 'But I hate the thought of just being a stand-in for Melinda.'

'I can assure you that you're not, and never will be, a stand-in for *anyone*. It happens to be *you* I want.'

'Isn't that because I'm the only woman here?' she asked defiantly.

Curtly, he denied, 'No, it isn't. If you don't believe me, you can walk out now.'

As her lips parted, he said flatly, 'You'll find the door isn't locked. That was just a pretence.'

Getting to his feet, he moved to allow her space. 'If you want to go, this is your chance.'

Scrambling off the bed, she headed for the door and turned the knob. It opened, confirming the truth of his words.

There was nothing to stop her leaving.

But did she *really* want to?

She had been fighting herself more than him, but why keep on fighting when, as he'd already remarked, they were both free?

He was the only man she had ever truly loved. The only

man she would ever love. He didn't love her, but then he hadn't loved Melinda...

And he'd said all she could have hoped to hear—*'It happens to be you I want...'*

So what was she to do? Walk away and congratulate herself on how strong she'd been? Or snatch the brief happiness of a night spent in his arms?

Common sense said walk away. One night of bliss would only make her future seem greyer and emptier.

But it would be grey and empty anyway, so why not have something wonderful to remember? For she didn't doubt it *would* be wonderful...

Closing the door carefully, she turned to look at him.

His expression held triumph, and some other emotion she was unable to identify.

'Decided to stay?' he asked softly.

Determined he shouldn't crow, she said, 'You offered to take my mind off things, and on reflection it seemed a better option than just lying awake worrying.'

He grimaced. 'That effectively puts me in the same category as all-night television or a good book. Come here, woman...'

She obeyed, her body pliant in his arms.

He lifted her face to his. 'The very least you can do is give me a kiss to assuage my hurt feelings.'

'Well, if it's only a kiss you want...' she said as flippantly as possible, while her heart beat a rapid tattoo against her ribs.

'I shall want a great deal more than that, but it will do for a start...'

While he kissed her, his tongue touched hers, searching and tormenting, fusing the kiss and sending shivers of desire running through her.

His free hand slid inside her robe, his warm fingers caressing her soft curves until he felt her response through the thin satin of her nightdress. Then one hand moved to cradle the back of her head, while the other untied the belt of her robe and eased it off.

Kissing and nibbling his way along her jawline and down the length of her slender neck, he slipped the nightdress straps from her shoulders. A second later he sent it to join the pool of satin at their feet, before his mouth found the warm hollow at the base of her throat.

The exquisite sensations he was evoking made her feel giddy, as if the entire world was swaying, and with an incoherent murmur she clung to him.

Raising his dark head, he looked at her dazed face, with its parted lips and closed eyes, then he stooped and lifted her on to the bed, to continue his sensual assault.

As well as a crimson and gold canopy, the carved four-poster had a luxurious mattress and soft pillows. Old and new going hand in hand. But the knowledge that Melinda had shared this bed suddenly intruded on Fran's bliss, making her feel far from comfortable.

Stretched by her side beneath the light duvet, naked flesh to naked flesh, Blaze was exploring the seductive curve of her breast when something about her stillness made him pause.

Studying her troubled face, he asked with his usual perception, 'What's bothering you?'

'Nothing,' she mumbled.

'Don't lie to me. I know something is. I can sense the tension. So what is it?'

When she hesitated, he said, 'Don't worry, I think I know. You're wondering if Melinda ever slept in this bed?'

'Yes,' Fran admitted.

'Well, if it makes you feel any better, she didn't. I always went to her room. Now, as I don't relish making love to a woman whose mind is on other things, if you would give me your full and undivided attention...?'

'I'll be only too happy to.'

'In that case I think I can promise you'll enjoy yourself. As you haven't been in my bed for over three years, and I need to make up for lost time, I intend to…' His lips brushing her ear, he whispered his intentions.

While she listened, a liquid core of heat formed in the pit of her stomach, and her nipples firmed betrayingly.

When his mouth found the evidence of her arousal, he gave a little murmur of satisfaction and proceeded to make shudders of ecstasy run through her.

A pearly grey dawn was filtering into the room when Fran opened her eyes. Blaze was lying beside her, one hand thrown over his head in an attitude of abandon, his fingers, with their neatly trimmed nails, curling into his palm.

From a mind drugged with sleep and pleasure she recalled that his promise of delight had been more than kept, and her stomach clenched at the thought of his passionate and inventive lovemaking. He knew just where to touch, where to apply a little pressure to heighten and prolong every sensation.

Afterwards, thoroughly sated, and too exhausted to worry about anything, she had slept like a baby in his arms.

Now it was his turn to sleep like a babe.

Propping herself on one elbow, she looked down at him, drinking in the sight of that beloved face, memorising this moment for when he had gone and she had nothing left to warm herself with but memories.

His ironic eyes were hidden, and his bony nose and tumbled hair gave him a strangely boyish look, in spite of the dark stubble adorning his jaw. The thick lashes, seeming out of place on such a very masculine face, were so long and curly that she was forced to envy them, and his mouth, with its exciting combination of austereness and sensuality, always made her heart beat faster…

As though her scrutiny had disturbed his slumber, he stirred. Without opening his eyes he felt for her with his hand and, pulling her down on top of him, murmured a long, interrogative, 'Mmm?'

'Mmm!' Fran answered.

He opened his eyes and smiled at her. Then, with a sudden swift movement she was unprepared for, he reversed their positions. Bending his head, he kissed her, and said, 'That's good, because I plan to do it all over again.'

When she awoke for the second time she was alone in the big bed, and there wasn't a sound. A glance at her watch showed it was almost one-thirty.

Sleeping through the morning was getting to be a habit, she thought ruefully.

Her body still felt languidly fulfilled and glowing with remembered ecstasy, but her mind, starting to grapple with hard, unpalatable facts, wasn't nearly so euphoric.

No matter what Blaze had said about wanting *her*, in the cold light of day Fran was convinced that almost any woman would have done to take Melinda's place.

If he'd cared in the slightest for her...

But the knowledge that he didn't had made sharing his bed bittersweet, and had brought almost as much pain as pleasure. As she had known it would do.

One-sided loving was like a knife turning in the heart. Every minute she stayed close to Blaze, every time he made love to her, only served to drive the blade that much deeper.

She had to get away, had to leave Balantyne Hall as soon as possible...

Reaching for her robe, which along with her nightdress had been picked up and placed tidily over a chair, she pulled it on, and, seeing the bathroom was empty, headed for the living room.

That too was empty, but the curtains had been drawn

back and a bright fire burnt in the grate to combat the cool-ness of the storm-washed September day.

Propped on the bureau, where the necklace had been, was a note in Blaze's forceful hand. 'Going to town. Expect to be back in time for lunch.' Then, scrawled on the bottom, a repressive, 'Don't even *think* of leaving.'

Her case was still standing where he'd left it, and, pick-ing it up, she carried it through to the bathroom.

Having cleaned her teeth and stripped off her robe, she removed Blaze's ring and put it carefully on one of the vanity units before stepping under the shower.

When she was dried and dressed, as though it was the most natural thing in the world, she found herself replacing the ring.

As she started to brush out her long hair, all the worries she had been striving to keep at bay began to crowd in on her relentlessly.

How could the necklace possibly be a fake? And had Melinda and Kirk really run off together?

It seemed unbelievable...

Fran was coiling her thick, silky hair into a knot when she heard the bedroom door open and Blaze's voice call sharply, 'Francesca?'

The hairpins she was holding in her mouth—a teenage practice deplored by her mother—prevented her from an-swering immediately.

She was thrusting in the last of the pins when the bath-room door was flung open and Blaze appeared on the threshold, looking both angry and alarmed.

He must have noticed her case was missing, Fran reali-sed, and, with everywhere being quiet, jumped to the con-clusion that she had ignored his warning and somehow managed to slip away.

For a split second his face registered relief at seeing her there, before a shutter came down. Then, his manner cool and impersonal, he informed her, 'I've asked for some lunch to be sent up, so as soon as you're ready...'

'I'll be out in just a minute.'

When she went through to the living room he was sitting by the fire. A loaded tray was waiting on the table.

As she took the chair opposite, he remarked, 'You must be hungry, so I suggest we get our food while it's hot. Would you like to start with some soup?'

She shook her head, and, having accepted a piece of quiche and some salad, picked up her knife and fork. Happening to glance up, she noticed his eyes were fixed on the ring.

Answering her uncertainty, he said quickly, 'I'm pleased to see you're still wearing it.'

The quiche was delicious, but with so much on her mind Fran's appetite had totally deserted her, and she had to make an effort to force it down.

As soon as their coffee cups were empty she turned to Blaze and asked anxiously, 'Is there any news?'

'It's confirmation rather than news. And from your point of view none of it's good.'

Bracing herself, she said quietly, 'Then you'd better tell me the worst.'

Leaning back, he stretched his long legs. 'Though I was certain Richard couldn't be mistaken about the necklace, the first thing I did when I got to town this morning was make a private visit to Al Cockburn, my insurance assessor.'

'And it *is* a fake?'

'Undoubtedly.'

Despite the fact that she hadn't held out much hope, Fran felt as though she'd been kicked in the stomach.

Helplessly, she said, 'I didn't know. Truly I didn't.'

'I believe you. I was watching your face while Richard was doing his stuff. There was no trace of guilt or awareness, and I'm sure there would have been if you *had* known.'

She took a deep, steadying breath. 'I still can't really credit it. I mean…it just doesn't seem possible. William Bailey is the most honest man I've ever met. He would *never* have been a party to such a thing.'

'What if he didn't know?'

Though the last thing she wanted to do was implicate William, honesty made Fran shake her head. 'He's been a goldsmith dealing with precious stones for over forty years, so surely he would have realised if he'd been given fake rubies to reset?'

Voicing a thought that had occurred to her the previous evening, she added flatly, '*You* must have guessed they were fake, otherwise you wouldn't have asked for Mr Henderson's opinion.'

'Though I distrusted the whole set-up from the word go, Varley might have got away with it for a while longer if I hadn't had a direct tip-off. You remember the phone call I received during dinner on Friday night? Well, the anonymous caller suggested then that fake stones had been made. When I asked him why he was taking the trouble to warn me, he said, "Because I owe that b…Varley one. He stole my wife."

'Yesterday morning I went to town, intending to get the necklace checked out…'

So that was why he'd been carrying it.

'But Cockburn wasn't there and I didn't want to waste any time. That's when I thought of Richard. The rest followed on logically. As soon as I knew there was a good chance that the necklace was a fake, and neither Melinda nor Varley had turned up here, I began to get the picture.

'I'd realized from the first that Melinda didn't like some of the clauses in our marriage contract, but rather than lose the chance of being a rich man's wife she'd gone along with them...

'*You* said you would stick by Varley if he was made penniless, but Melinda isn't like that at all. She cares about money. I always knew that if *I* lost everything I had, she would probably go too. At the moment, however, I'm wealthy enough to provide whatever she wants, so I couldn't see her giving it all up to be with a man who, however much she might fancy him, was on the verge of bankruptcy.

'But a man with rubies worth millions in his possession was a different proposition.'

Her voice just above a whisper, Fran asked, 'So you think Melinda knew about the fakes?'

'Oh, she knew all right.'

Something about his conviction made her ask, 'You don't think they planned this together?'

'That's exactly what I think. In her own way, Melinda is just as unscrupulous as Varley...'

Yes, she could well believe that, Fran thought.

'And as neither of them liked the idea of being poor,' Blaze continued, 'they decided to do something about it.'

Her voice not quite steady, Fran asked, 'Then you're absolutely *certain* they've run off together?'

Noting the quiver, he answered more gently, 'I'm afraid so.'

All at once fiercely glad, Fran felt her eyes fill with tears. Though Blaze didn't know it, he'd had a lucky escape. Melinda's stated intention of reneging on the marriage contact would only have brought discord and unhappiness.

At least now he had a chance of finding another woman who would give him the children he wanted...

Seeing Blaze's eyes fixed on her, Fran looked hastily away, trying not to blink. She was forced to, and in spite of all her efforts twin tears overflowed and rolled down her cheeks in tracks of shiny wetness.

'Damn Varley!' Blaze said harshly. Getting to his feet, he pulled her into his arms, murmuring, 'Don't cry... Don't cry...'

His concern, coming on top of everything else, was her undoing, and she began to weep in earnest.

Cradling her head against his chest, his mouth buried in her hair, Blaze held her until the sobs had died away.

Regaining control, and ashamed of her show of weakness, Fran lifted her head and prepared to leave the comfort of his arms.

Looking down at her, he wiped away the tears with his thumbs, before letting her sink back into the chair.

'I know you think you love him, but, believe me, he's not worth crying over. Sooner or later you'll have to face the fact that he's no good. From the start I was sure he was up to something, and for a while I thought you might well be a part of it. Now I'm satisfied that Varley was just using you, and quite ruthlessly.'

As she opened her mouth to protest he added firmly, 'No, I'm not just guessing. I'm one hundred per cent certain.'

CHAPTER EIGHT

'How can you be so sure?'

Blaze spread expressive hands. 'Start from the beginning and work it out for yourself. You saw Melinda and Varley together. How did they get on?'

'Very well,' Fran admitted. 'Kirk was charming to her and she responded, but I presumed that...'

'That it was just a good business relationship?'

'Yes.'

'Obviously it was a great deal more. My guess is that from the word go there was an instant and powerful attraction between the pair of them. I was safely in the States, so they began seeing each other—which would explain why she stayed up in Manchester so much. I did wonder about that...

'Then one or other of them must have had the bright idea of stealing the rubies, and they began to plan how best to do it without anyone finding out. The first thing would have been to have a set of fake stones made—only as you yourself pointed out, William Bailey—whom I believe to be an honest man—would almost certainly have spotted them. To get over that problem they decided to have two necklaces made.'

'Two?'

'It was the only thing that made sense. I rang William Bailey this morning and he confirmed that he had made two identical gold settings. As soon as he was given the design and the dimensions he made a trial one, so to speak, which was handed over to Melinda for her approval. He was told that Miss Ross was very happy with it, but she wanted to keep it to show me. Therefore, on Varley's instructions, he made a second one, in which he set the real rubies.

'In the meantime the fake stones were put into the first setting, probably by one of Varley's shady friends, so all that was needed was for him to make a last-minute switch.

'You yourself told me that before Varley "left for Amsterdam" he packed the necklace up himself and put it in the safe. Then the following day, just before your taxi arrived to take you to the airport, William Bailey opened the safe and gave you the package. At that stage neither of you had any reason to doubt that it contained the real necklace.

'Melinda and Varley are both clever,' Blaze went on, a hint of admiration in his tone, 'and the whole thing was planned with the greatest care. *She* made certain that you and Varley were invited to the Hall, and *he* made certain that *you* were carrying the necklace. Your total innocence was to be their trump card.'

'I don't—'

'You admitted that Varley showed no interest in you until you got the go-ahead to redesign the setting?'

Fran nodded.

'But he's a man of the world. He must have noticed *your* interest in *him*?'

She flushed uncomfortably. 'I suppose so.'

'When did he actually propose?'

Slowly, she said, 'When he was outlining his plan for delivering the necklace and he first suggested that I should carry it. I considered it was much too big a responsibility for someone who was only an employee, and I told him so...

'He said something like, "My darling girl, you must know that I don't think of you as a mere employee. In fact I was about to ask you to become part of the firm... Yes, I really do mean marry me..."'

Blaze nodded grimly. 'Everything depended on you carrying the necklace, so he'd have promised you the moon if he'd thought it necessary. And to add weight to his proposal, and allay any faint doubts you might have had, he asked you to move in with him.

'Meanwhile he'd set up this trip to Amsterdam, and made arrangements for you to meet him at the airport on his return. That done, he fixed for one of his underworld associates to follow you to London, well clear of his home ground, before putting the rest of his plan into operation.

'His message about being delayed was an essential part of the strategy. He needed you to be alone—but somewhere nice and public, like a taxi rank at an airport—when your bag was snatched. That way he would have an excellent alibi for himself, and the only thing the firm could have been accused of was some degree of negligence. Though the secrecy angle was quite a valid one.

'His plans must have appeared to be working smoothly until, when he was about to board the plane for Amsterdam, he either discovered or strongly suspected that he was being followed.

'Though he couldn't have been sure who was following him, or why, afraid of things going wrong, he changed his mind about leaving for Amsterdam and set out to give his shadow the slip...

'As you know, he succeeded, and once more his plans seemed all set to work. You were given the necklace, caught the plane to London, waited for him as instructed, and then when he was "delayed" went to get a taxi...

'Everything had gone like clockwork until your bag was snatched, but then, instead of you having hysterics and reporting it, as he'd expected, you got quietly into a taxi and carried on to Balantyne Hall.

'His plan was brilliant, in its way, and no doubt would have worked if you hadn't made up your mind to wear the necklace instead of carrying it. That unexpected decision threw a spanner in the works.'

Bewildered, she said, 'But if he'd gone to all the trouble to have a fake necklace made, why was it necessary to steal it?'

'That was the whole purpose. He couldn't afford to try and palm me off with a fake. He knew it wouldn't be too long before someone spotted it, and then the fat would be in the fire.'

'I still don't follow... If the whole purpose was simply to steal it, why not leave just a weighted box?'

'Too risky. William Bailey might possibly have made a last-minute check. If he had, without a close examination, the fake was good enough to pass muster.'

'I see,' she breathed.

'Then, once it was safely stolen, in a manner of speaking, no one would know it had been a fake. Both you and William Bailey would have been convinced it was the real thing. And in the unlikely event of it ever being recovered, who's to say that the criminal who stole it hadn't made the switch?

'All that Varley and Melinda needed to do was sit tight until the furore had died down. If things had gone according to plan Melinda would no doubt have come on to the Hall. But some time over the weekend, and certainly before the wedding, she would have found some pretext to back out of the agreement and end our engagement. Then, with all the worry and stress of having the necklace stolen, it would have been easy for Varley to pick a quarrel with you and break things off. When they eventually did get together, even if someone was suspicious, no blame could be attached to two people for simply falling in love.

'Everything must have seemed cut and dried, and it no doubt came as a very nasty shock when the necklace wasn't in your bag and the whole scheme fell apart... In fact I strongly suspect that at first they were thrown into a panic…'

'Do you think that's why they made the mistake of going to Kirk's apartment?'

'I'm fairly sure they must have had some pressing reason to risk going back there. Possibly it was to pick up his passport, or perhaps the real necklace… If it was either or both of those, it seems on the cards that they're planning to make a run for it.

'Of course they won't know how long they've got before someone puts two and two together and the fake is discovered… Though it's early days yet, so with a bit of luck they'll still be feeling relatively secure.'

'You don't think they'll realise that they've been picked up again?'

'Though they must have been extremely wary, I doubt it.' Grimly, he added, 'After getting blasted for their previous poor showing, Ritters have got a team of top men and women following them.'

'So you know where they are?'

'The last I heard they appeared to be heading for London.'

'What do you intend to do?'

'Nothing, at the moment. I'm waiting to see which way they jump. If they *are* going to try and leave the country, then they'll almost certainly have the necklace with them. It's a big risk, of course, but one they have to take…

'On the other hand if they're intending to lie low—and London is a good place to disappear in—the necklace may be stashed away somewhere. Which could make recovering it a great deal more difficult.'

Fran moistened her dry lips. 'What if you don't get it back? I suppose it's insured?'

'It's insured up to the hilt, but in the circumstances I

wouldn't expect any insurance company to pay out. They'll no doubt argue that insufficient care was taken.'

'I'm sorry,' she said helplessly.

'Financially I'm well able to stand the loss.' His voice steely, he added, 'But I don't want to lose a family heirloom, and I dislike being made a fool of.'

'Who doesn't?'

Hearing the bitterness, he remarked, 'In your case they didn't succeed. It was your resourcefulness that turned the tables.'

She could only be glad that he looked at it that way. At least it made things easier.

Bracing herself, she took the bull by the horns. 'Now you're happy that I'm not to blame in any way, I'd like to leave as soon as possible.'

'Why?'

The question took her by surprise. 'Well, I—'

'What is there to hurry back for? You have no lover waiting for you, no job, not even a bedsitter to go back to.'

'Well, that's just it... I—I need to get my life sorted out. Once I've found somewhere to live and another job—'

'In the circumstances that might not be easy.'

Hoping his words held no veiled threat, and striving to sound confident, she said, 'Starting all over again isn't so bad. I've done it before.'

His voice searing, he informed her, '*You* may find the idea of starting all over again reasonable. *I* don't.'

'But neither of us have much option,' she pointed out shakily.

'I'm not sure I agree there. In most situations there's usually more than one course open. For instance, with regard to the theft of the Balantyne rubies, I have the choice of either dealing with it myself or calling in the police.'

'The police?' All the colour drained from her face.

'Theft, or even attempted theft, is against the law,' he pointed out.

'But if you can get the necklace back, surely it won't be necessary to involve the police?'

His eyes on her face, he asked curtly, 'Can you give me one good reason why I shouldn't?'

Stammering a little, she admitted, 'I w-wouldn't like either Melinda or Kirk to go to gaol because of me.'

'It wouldn't be because of you.'

'Perhaps not, but I hate the idea of—'

'So you think that when I catch up with them I should give them a pat on the head and say how clever they've been, and what a pity they didn't quite pull it off?'

Flushing, she said, 'No, of course not, but I—'

'You still love Varley and you can't bear to think of him in prison?'

Blaze sounded so angry that Fran bit her lip and wished she'd stayed silent.

'Personally I think he deserves to be behind bars.'

'What about Melinda?'

'They were in this together. To reverse an old saying, "What's sauce for the gander…"'

Fran shivered. 'Then you do intend to tell the police?'

His shoulders moved in a slight shrug. 'I may decide not to press charges. It all depends.'

'On what?'

'You.'

'Me?' Grey-green eyes cloudy and confused, she said, 'I—I don't understand. How can it depend on me?'

'It's a question of how co-operative you're prepared to be. As I told you last night, I think you owe me.'

'But I did as you asked…I did everything you asked… And you've just made it plain that you don't blame me for what happened.'

'I don't *blame* you, but the fact remains that you were a

party to it, and you are the only one available to make some reparation.'

'But surely there's a good chance you'll get the necklace back?'

'It isn't the necklace that concerns me...'

As she stared at him, a sudden premonition making her heart start to beat with slow, heavy thuds, he added, 'I have a wedding arranged for tomorrow, and I don't like the idea of all my plans being wrecked.'

She fought against the knowledge. 'You don't mean...?'

'That's exactly what I mean.'

'No, I won't... I *can't*...' she cried wildly. 'We don't love each other—'

Brutally, he said, 'You loved Varley, and where has that got you? And I thought I'd made it plain that I don't regard love as a necessary ingredient of a good, stable marriage. As I told you previously, I want a partner who is compatible and basically good-tempered; someone warm and passionate, with enough spice to make life interesting. Don't you want all those things?'

Yes, she did. But she also wanted love.

His eyes on her face, he continued, 'You have all the qualities I've been looking for.'

'I'm not beautiful, like Melinda.'

'In your own way you're even more beautiful. You have a kind of sweetness, an inner radiance she lacks.'

'I'm not sexy, like her.'

'I'll be the judge of that.'

'You might find me dull compared to her.'

'Though Melinda rated high for fun and excitement, and was more...adventurous, I've no worries about finding you dull. I'm sure you'll make an intelligent, stimulating companion, as well as a wife who will keep her wedding vows and help to make a happy home for our children. In fact in those respects I'm convinced you're more suitable than Melinda.

'In return, I'll try my hardest to make you a good husband. I can give you every material thing you could wish for—'

'I don't care a jot about material things,' she broke in hoarsely.

As if she hadn't spoken, he went on, 'You'll have a chance to travel and do everything you've always wanted to do... And sexually we're well-suited, to say the very least, so I'm sure I can keep you happy in bed.

'Think about it. Isn't it better than being alone? Better than trying to find a cheap bedsit and another job? Better than trying to start all over again, knowing the man you love is in prison and you've helped to put him there...?'

'But you just said it wouldn't be because of me.'

'In that sense it won't. But the fact that you could buy his immunity from prosecution by—'

Agitation brought her to her feet. 'By marrying a man I loathe?'

She saw his jaw clench, and he too rose, seeming to tower over her.

With scorching derision, he said, 'Of course, if the sacrifice is too great, you could always wait for Varley to come out of prison and beg him to take you back. Melinda won't want a penniless gaolbird, so you may be lucky...'

Without conscious volition, Fran's hand came up and gave that mocking face a stinging slap.

She had never struck anyone in her life before, had never thought of herself as a violent person, but her blow had been hard enough to jerk his head back and make him blink.

He stood quite still, while Fran, horrified by what she'd done, stared at the red mark that had appeared on his tanned cheek.

'Well, well, well,' he said softly. 'I didn't know you had it in you.' Then, his hand going up to gingerly feel his face, he added ruefully, 'For someone who looks so inoffensive, you certainly pack a wallop.'

'I'm sorry,' she whispered.

'There's no need to apologise,' he told her. 'You had plenty of provocation.'

Deeply ashamed, she said, 'I still shouldn't have done what I did,' and, unable to help herself, began to tremble violently.

Blaze took her in his arms and held her close, one hand moving soothingly up and down her spine. 'It's all right...I was asking for it. There's no need to be upset.'

His ready forgiveness, his generosity of spirit, made her feel even more ashamed, and she had to fight to hold back the tears.

Lifting her head, she looked into his face, and, standing on tiptoe to touch her lips to his burning cheek, assured him shakily, 'I promise I won't do it again.'

'You may need to from time to time, just to keep me in my place.' Humorously, he added, 'So long as you're not going to turn into a husband-beater...'

She made a little sound, half-laugh, half-sob.

'And you always kiss me better...

'Now then,' His hands closed lightly on her upper arms as he became suddenly businesslike. 'I suggest we start for town more or less straight away and spend the night at the Empire Park. That way we'll have time to do a little shopping before the wedding, which is scheduled for four o'clock...'

Though his manner held no trace of doubt, he was watching her narrowly. His dark eyes had a guarded, waiting look, and she knew he wasn't anywhere near as confident as he'd sounded.

But she was emotionally drained, her opposition over, defeated.

It had nothing to do with Melinda and Kirk. She couldn't believe that Blaze would deliberately put either of them behind bars. But suddenly she didn't want to start all over again, alone and lonely. She didn't want to lose the man she loved for the second time.

Marrying him, when he cared nothing for her, was taking an enormous risk. She recalled what he himself had said about one-sided loving. *'To be steered clear of at all costs! It unbalances a relationship and can only cause trouble when one partner wants more than the other can give...'*

But if she kept her love a secret—and while he thought she still loved Kirk that should be easy—surely between them they could make the marriage work?

Even if pain went hand in hand with pleasure, and despair sometimes swamped delight, loving him as she did, living *with* him had to be infinitely better than living *without* him.

Becoming aware that he was still waiting for a response, his lean face taut, she admitted her surrender by asking, 'But won't there be difficulties? Over the wedding, I mean?'

She heard his short, sharp sigh of relief, before he said, 'As I'd applied for, and been granted, a special licence, the only thing necessary was to alter the name of the bride. That I did yesterday, while you were getting ready for the party.'

'Then this was already *planned*! You must have been very sure I'd agree.' Her voice held more than a touch of bitterness.

'Hardly,' he answered drily. 'But you know what they say: Faint heart never won fair lady...'

'*Won* hardly seems to be the appropriate word.'

'You consider *coerced* would more apposite?'

'Wouldn't it?'

'Though I feel sure you'd hate to see Varley languishing in prison, I don't believe that was what...shall we say...swayed you?'

'Oh?'

'I think, possibly at some subconscious level, you *want* to marry me.'

What if he'd guessed the truth? Feeling hollow inside, she asked, 'What makes you think that?'

'For one thing you kept the ring on... And for another there's a strong sexual bond between us, and has been since we first laid eyes on each other.'

He tipped her face up to his and looked into her eyes. 'You may loathe me, but you still *want* me.'

'I don't loathe you,' she said in a small voice.

He smiled. 'Then there's hope for us yet.'

After spending some time downstairs in his study, apparently making and receiving phone calls, Blaze put their small amount of luggage into the car and they set off for London.

It was a fine, bright day, and after an easy drive they reached Mayfair by early evening, and took what Blaze quizzically described as 'the scenic route' to Abercrombie Square.

Noting that the surroundings were familiar, without thinking, Fran remarked, 'Isn't your flat somewhere near here?' Then, recalling the nights she'd spent there, she found herself blushing furiously.

Blaze slanted her an amused glance. 'Yes, it's just a bit further on. I'm pleased to see you remember it...'

The attractive little corner flat on Green Lane had overlooked some leafy gardens and an old grey church. A quiet backwater in the centre of town, it had been a favourite of Blaze's, and she was wondering why they weren't staying there instead of a hotel when he added casually, 'I decided not to keep it.'

Seeing her surprise, he explained, 'Somehow a service flat, however pleasant, never seems like home, so I ended the lease when I went back to the States.'

He turned down Abercrombie Street and into the square, and while she was still puzzling over his stated reason for giving up the flat they drew up outside the dignified entrance of the Empire Park.

Blaze tossed the car keys to a uniformed garage attendant, and a moment later the manager, a pleasant-looking man in his fifties, appeared to greet them by name and personally usher them up to the penthouse suite.

Two bell-boys followed behind, one with their small amount of luggage, the other with a bottle of champagne in an ice bucket and two long-stemmed crystal glasses.

The suite was quietly palatial, with an elegant sitting room and two large bedrooms separated by a dressing room. From the sitting room sliding glass panels opened on to a roofed terrace, screened by a lattice-work grille.

When the manager and his minions had taken their leave, Blaze looked at the two pieces of luggage which had been placed side by side in the master bedroom, and with a slightly mocking gleam in his eyes asked, 'Are you happy with this arrangement?' Before she had a chance to reply, he went on, 'Or would you like to observe the proprieties until we're married?'

'You mean separate rooms?'

'As I'd like us to share a room when we're married, this could well be your last chance to sleep alone.' As she hesitated, he added, 'The choice is yours.' But it was obvious he had no doubt of her answer.

Feeling a sudden urge to deflate his ego, she said sweetly, 'In that case, I'll take this opportunity to be alone.'

'Very well.' If he was at all put out, he didn't show it.

Picking up her case, he carried it through to the other bedroom.

Then, glancing at his watch, he suggested, 'We've plenty of time before dinner, so how about a spot of decadence?'

Cautiously, she said, 'It rather depends what you mean by decadence.'

He gave her a mocking grin. 'Nothing very terrible. Just a glass of champagne in the Jacuzzi.'

'Do we have a Jacuzzi?'

'There's one on the terrace.'

'I haven't got a bathing costume.'

'You won't need a bathing costume. It's shielded from every direction, and quite private.' Seeing she was about to refuse, he raised a dark brow. 'Too daring for you?'

Stung by the taunt, and remembering his remark about Melinda being more adventurous, she said, 'Not at all. Give me a couple of minutes.'

Fran took off her clothes and put on a white towelling robe that was hanging in the bathroom before venturing on to the terrace.

To the left, marble steps led down to a sunken area with mosaic-type tiles that reminded her of a Roman bath-house. In the centre was a Jacuzzi, from which steam was rising gently.

She had hoped to be the first in, but, his towelling robe hanging over a convenient rail, Blaze was already seated on the bench that ran around the bath, bubbling water up to his chest.

Still oddly shy, in spite of everything, she saw with relief that his head was back and his heavy lids were closed, the dark lashes lying on his hard cheeks.

Barefoot and silent, she took off her own robe and hung it next to Blaze's, before turning to go down the steps.

With something of a shock she saw that his eyes were

open and he was studying her slim body and long, shapely legs with undisguised interest and admiration.

Feeling her colour start to rise betrayingly, she kept her head high and, gathering her composure round her like a cloak, walked slowly down the pale marble steps and into the hot water.

He held out a hand, and when she took it pulled her down beside him. 'Bravo,' he applauded softly. 'You certainly don't lack spirit... And your figure is even better than I remember.'

Red as a poppy, she made no reply.

'Champagne?' He turned to reach behind him, where the bottle was waiting. Easing off the cork with a pop, he filled two glasses with the smoking wine and handed her one, before lifting his own in a toast. 'To us!'

'To us,' she echoed.

They sipped in silence, the combination of hot bubbling water and cold bubbling wine a strangely potent one.

When their glasses were empty, Blaze returned them both to the tray. As he did so his arm lightly brushed against her breast, and she caught her breath.

She saw by his small, satisfied smile that he was well aware of her reaction.

Leaning her head back against the padded rest, she closed her eyes and tried to relax while the underwater jets, at once soothing and invigorating, massaged her torso and limbs. Blaze sat quietly, making no further effort to talk. But, very aware of his supple, naked body beside her, it was several minutes before some of Fran's tension began to slacken.

He on the other hand seemed to be totally at ease, his breathing light and even. A surreptitious glance from beneath her long lashes proved that his eyes were closed once more.

She had just decided that he was asleep when he moved

a fraction, and the length of his muscular thigh touched hers.

Stiffening, she was about to inch away when some instinct warned that he was only pretending to be asleep, and was intent on teasing her.

Determined not to be teased, she stayed where she was, while every nerve-ending in her body zinged into life.

After perhaps thirty seconds, with a sound halfway between a laugh and a groan, he admitted, 'Okay, you win.' Then, ruefully, 'Hoist with my own petard.' Taking her hand he put it on his firm flesh, trapping it there.

'Serves you right,' she said with malicious satisfaction.

'Now that's what I call heartless.' His eyes on her breasts, he added, 'However, I'd hazard a guess that *you're* not totally unaffected.'

When, unable to deny it, she stayed silent, with a gleam in his eye he suggested softly, 'We've time to do something about it before dinner, if you like?'

She shook her head. 'I'd prefer to observe the proprieties until we're married, as we agreed.'

Sighing, he released her.

Absurdly disappointed that he'd taken her at her word, she said, 'You mentioned half an hour. It must be all of that, and I'm beginning to feel hungry. So if you don't mind I think I'll start to get ready.'

'By all means,' he agreed politely.

She got to her feet and, aware that he was watching her, made as dignified a retreat as possible.

Pulling on the towelling robe, she belted it securely before turning to ask, 'Are we eating in the hotel?'

He followed her out of the bath, water pouring down his long, straight legs, and, shrugging into his own robe, shook his head. 'I was thinking of taking you to the Medici.'

Fran knew that the Medici, which was quite close to Park

Lane, was rated as one of the top London restaurants, and her heart sank.

'Have you already booked?' she asked anxiously.

'No.'

'Will you be able to get a table this late?'

His voice casual, he answered, 'I think so.'

Though he'd said *think*, she knew he must be quite certain.

'Only I've really nothing to wear,' she admitted.

'What about the cocktail dress you wore on Friday? That looked quite charming.'

With a clear picture in her mind of Melinda's wardrobe, with its rail of elegant designer dresses, Fran said in a rush, 'It's not very posh...I—I don't want you to be ashamed of me.'

'I won't be ashamed of you.'

Forced to be content with that assurance, she went through to her bedroom, and, opening her case, took out the dress.

It was off the peg and inexpensive, but at least the material was the uncrushable variety, and it had a lined stole which would serve as an evening cloak.

Having dressed and made up with care, she studied herself in the full-length mirror and decided that, though she was no match for Melinda, she would pass muster.

The stole over her arm, she went back to the living room to find that Blaze, wearing a well-cut evening jacket, was standing by the window waiting.

Though her feet were quite silent on the thick carpet he turned at her approach, making her wonder whether he had some kind of sixth sense.

His eyes travelling slowly over her, from the smooth chignon, which emphasised her pure bone structure, to her slim silk-clad ankles, he nodded in silent approval.

Then, taking the stole, he moved behind her to put it

around her shoulders, at the same time stooping to touch his lips to the vulnerable spot where her neck and shoulder joined.

The caress made a little shiver run through her, and heightened the sexual tension which still gripped them both.

One of his hands went round her waist to draw her against him while the other slid beneath her chin and tilted her head back. His mouth was only inches from hers when his mobile phone began to bleep.

He muttered, 'Damn!' and, straightening, drew it from his pocket.

Moving away, she watched his face as he answered curtly, 'Balantyne... Yes... Yes, I see... Where...? You're quite sure...? Excellent... Yes, I'll be there... Twenty minutes... Half an hour at the most...'

His grey eyes were bright, the set of his dark head alert, and she could sense both a leashed excitement and a steely purpose behind his quietly controlled manner.

Dropping the small phone back into his pocket, he said, 'I hope you don't mind, but our dinner venue has changed.'

'No, I don't mind at all,' she assured him, and waited for him to tell her where they were going and why the change of plan.

But with no further explanation he hurried her out of the penthouse, across the luxurious foyer, and into the lift.

CHAPTER NINE

THEY were just crossing the main lobby when a taxi drew up outside to deposit some guests.

'Just what we need,' Blaze said with satisfaction. He signalled to the driver, gave an address Fran didn't catch and, having handed her in, jumped in beside her.

As they headed west, he added, 'This will be more convenient than taking the car.'

'Where are we going?' she asked.

'The Royal George. It's a small hotel not far from Kensington High Street.'

He didn't volunteer any further information, and, though puzzled by the sudden change of location, she didn't ask for any.

As they headed for Kensington in the gathering dusk, shop windows made the pavements bright, and street lamps glowed orange against the deep blue of the sky. There were few pedestrians about, and even the traffic was fairly light.

The Royal George was in Newlands Street, a quiet cul-de-sac. Once a handsome private house, now a hotel with a porticoed entrance, it displayed a board with gold lettering advising that the Georgian Room was open to non-residents.

At first glance it didn't strike Fran as the kind of place that Blaze would favour, but clearly she was wrong.

Having helped her out of the taxi, he had a low-toned conversation with the driver before escorting her up the steps and across the wine-red carpeted lobby to the Georgian Room.

Its decor was early nineteen-hundreds and unappealing,

with dark walls and heavy lampshades, while the atmosphere was stifling in its respectability.

Fran wasn't in the least surprised to see that there were only two tables occupied.

One was close to the door, and as they walked past it a middle-aged couple—a woman with crimped grey hair and a balding man—paused in their discussion of what to have for dessert to glance up at them.

The other was at the far side of the room, in a gloomy alcove partially screened by a collection of dejected-looking aspidistras.

A hand beneath her elbow, Blaze led Fran across the room and over to the table in the alcove, where another couple were eating in silence.

Fran was still staring at the pair in stunned disbelief when Blaze said smoothly, 'Good evening. I hope you don't mind if we join you?'

The man and the woman looked up, startled. As both faces reflected shock and dismay Blaze added conversationally, 'I wouldn't have thought this place was quite your style.'

Melinda was easily the first to recover. 'Nor yours, Edward darling.'

Blaze smiled grimly. 'It seems we all had a special reason for coming here.'

Sitting quite still, his shoulders hunched defensively, Kirk looked for all the world like someone who had just received a fist in the solar plexus.

Melinda glanced from one man to the other, and with a poise that in the circumstances Fran was forced to admire, said coolly, 'I don't believe you two men have met. Kirk, this is Edward Balantyne...Edward, Kirk Varley...'

'Forgive me if I don't shake hands,' Blaze said, more than a hint of contempt in his voice.

Pulling out a chair, he pressed Fran into it before taking the remaining seat.

As he settled himself an elderly waiter appeared and presented them each with a menu. Having given his a cursory glance, Blaze looked up to ask, 'Is there anything you can recommend?'

Looking quite pleased to be consulted, the waiter suggested, 'At the moment we have a French chef whose speciality is Coquilles Saint-Jacques...'

'Francesca?' Blaze raised an enquiring brow.

Her voice having deserted her, she nodded.

'Coquilles Saint-Jacques it is, then, and a bottle of Pouilly-Fuissé.'

When the waiter had gone, Melinda, who seemed determined to treat the whole thing lightly, asked, 'So how did you know we'd be here?'

'How do you think?'

'Oh, dear! And we felt sure we'd given that odious little man the slip when we stopped at a service station. I guess there must have been more than one of them?'

'The agency was learning from past mistakes.'

'Why were you having us followed?'

'I'm sure I don't need to tell you.'

Carefully, she said, 'I presume you have the necklace?'

'Yes, it was delivered safely.'

'What do you think of it?'

'The design is beautiful. It's a pity the stones aren't real.'

She sighed. 'Kirk said it wouldn't take you long to spot a fake.' Then, looking at Fran for the first time, she asked, 'Just for curiosity, how *did* it come to be delivered safely?'

'I wasn't happy about carrying it.' To Fran's surprise, her voice sounded almost normal. 'So I decided to wear it.'

Jumping to his feet, Kirk snarled, 'You stupid little bitch! If you'd done as you were told, none of this would have happened. Why in hell's name couldn't you—?'

'That's enough!' Though quiet, Blaze's voice cracked like a whip. 'I'd strongly advise you to sit down.'

When the other man had sunk back into his seat, he added coldly, 'And mind what you're saying in future. If you speak to Francesca like that again, I'll break your neck.'

'There's no need to get angry, darling,' Melinda reproved him. 'You can't blame Kirk for being upset. All his plans have gone wrong, and frankly the whole thing has turned into a nightmare that I would rather not be involved in...'

Blaze gave her a straight look. 'I haven't the faintest doubt that you planned everything together. So it's a bit late to try and come the innocent.'

Melinda pouted at him prettily. 'Darling, how ungallant of you. And as a matter of fact it was...' She was interrupted by the waiter bringing a bottle of chilled Pouilly-Fuissé.

Almost as soon as Blaze had tried it, nodded his approval and indicated that four wine glasses were to be poured, the *coquilles* arrived.

'If you would like to carry on with your own meal?' he suggested to the others.

But no one, it seemed, had any appetite.

'I'd like to get out of this place.' For the first time Melinda sounded edgy. 'It gives me the heebie-jeebies. We only booked in here because Kirk thought somewhere like this would be safer than sitting around at the airport... *Safer*. That's a laugh!' she added bitterly.

'So when were you thinking of leaving?' Blaze enquired smoothly.

Kirk gave her a warning glance.

'Oh, what's the use of trying to kid ourselves?' she demanded irritably. 'You know as well as I do that the game's up.'

Raising her glass to Blaze, she took a sip, then, reverting to her former manner, said almost flippantly, 'We'd planned to leave very early in the morning for fresh fields and pastures new.'

'Such as?'

'Can't you guess?'

'South America?'

'Brazil. Rio de Janeiro, to be exact. I've always wanted to live and love in Rio.'

'How did you manage the fare?'

She grimaced ruefully. 'I'm afraid I was forced to part with your wedding present. I didn't get anywhere near what the Porsche was worth, but it would have been enough to tide us over until...'

'Until you could sell the rubies?'

She lifted slim shoulders in a shrug. 'I never could see the point of having precious stones that just lie in a bank vault.'

'Possibly not, but I must point out that they aren't yours to sell. They're part of a Balantyne family tradition—'

'But darling, you told me you'd lived most of your life in the States. I don't believe you give a hoot for the Balantyne family traditions.'

'That's where you're wrong. Having taken over the Balantyne estate I think the least I can do is carry on as my father would have wished.'

'How incredibly stuffy,' she scoffed. 'You don't really intend to follow things through to the letter, do you?'

'Yes.'

She widened her eyes. 'You're going to let your bride wear the rubies, and then, when the wedding's over, put them away for twenty years until the next generation want to marry?'

'That's exactly what I'm going to do,' he assured her icily.

Shrewdly, she changed tack. 'Well, if you feel so strongly about it, I'm sorry I wasn't there to wear them at the party as planned...'

When he made no comment, she went on, 'I suppose when you weren't able to produce either a fiancée or the rubies you had to cancel it?'

'Not at all. Everything went ahead as arranged.'

A flicker of surprise in her blue eyes, she asked, 'How did you explain my absence?'

'I didn't. As no one had ever met you, I simply found myself another fiancée.'

There was a brief silence, then, showing how quick-witted she was, Melinda looked at Fran and said considering-ly, 'I don't want to sound rude, but you don't look the kind that could carry it off—'

'There again you're wrong,' Blaze cut in evenly. 'Francesca carried it off magnificently.'

'And I suppose she wore the fake rubies?'

'They were good enough to pass muster.'

'So no one knows about...?' She let the question tail off.

'I haven't yet informed the police, if that's what you mean.'

At the mention of the word *police* Melinda's confidence faltered a little. 'I hope that won't be necessary?'

'It all depends.'

'On what?'

'On how quickly I get the rubies back, for one thing.'

Melinda's beautiful face took on a calculating look, and, making it quite obvious what she meant, she asked, 'Are the rubies the *only* thing you want back?'

There was a pregnant pause, and at least three of the people round the table held their breath.

Blaze's grey eyes flicked from one to another of the wait-ing faces before he answered calmly, 'No, they're not.'

Kirk lost colour; Fran, her heart feeling as though it was

being squeezed by a giant fist, stared blindly at her untouched plate; Melinda breathed an audible sigh of relief.

After a moment she asked slyly, 'Do I take it you haven't cancelled the wedding?'

'No, I haven't cancelled the wedding.'

'So if you were to get the rubies back straight away everything could go ahead as arranged...'

'It *could*,' he agreed. 'But in view of what's happened, I'm not—'

'I can understand how you feel,' she broke in hastily, 'and I really don't blame you for being angry.'

'That's nice of you.' The sarcasm was blistering.

'But as I tried to tell you earlier,' she persisted, 'the whole thing was Kirk's idea...'

Kirk made as if to protest, then fell silent, his fair, handsome face tired and beaten.

Looking at the wreck of the man she had once thought she loved, Fran could only feel sorry for him.

'If I'd had any sense I would never have gone along with it,' Melinda went on. 'But it was one of those sudden and powerful attractions, and I'm afraid I lost my head... I'm sorry now that I behaved so stupidly—'

'I bet you are.'

Brushing aside the interruption, she went on with the easy confidence of a woman sure of herself and her own beauty, 'But it's not too late. After all, there's no real harm been done, is there? So if you want to go on as if nothing has happened...?'

Before Blaze could speak, Kirk said, an ugly look appearing on his face, 'Just a word of warning. Before you decide to take her back, there's something you ought to know. Try asking her—'

Losing her cool, Melinda turned on him furiously. 'Why don't you keep out of this?'

Suddenly he was pleading. 'Don't go back to him, Mel...

You said you loved me... We're much better suited, and you know it...' He seized her hand. 'Everything I tried to do was for *us*...'

Pulling her hand free, she said trenchantly, 'You must be mad if you think I've the slightest intention of staying with a penniless bankrupt who could well end up in prison.'

'If I go to prison I'll take damn good care that I don't go alone—'

'Instead of making threats,' Blaze broke in curtly, 'suppose you tell me what you think I should be asking Melinda?'

'Ask her whether she ever really intended to have your children.'

Blaze's grey eyes narrowed on Melinda's beautiful, heart-shaped face. 'Well?'

'Of course I did, darling,' she assured him. 'You know quite well it was part of our contract, and I would have kept to it—'

'She's lying,' Kirk burst out hoarsely. Then, with something like desperation, '*You* tell him, Fran. You were there when she admitted she had no intention of ever having children.'

Blaze turned to look at Fran.

Feeling sick inside, she shook her head mutely. She wanted no part of it. If he was prepared to take Melinda back after all that had happened he must want her very badly indeed. And now he'd been warned it was up to him.

Melinda turned to Blaze, her smile blatantly triumphant. 'You see, darling? Kirk's jealous... He was just trying to make trouble.'

Reaching across the table, she put a possessive hand on Blaze's sleeve. 'Now, if you can forget about these last few days I'm prepared to go ahead and marry you as planned.'

His answering smile as glittering and dangerous as a

knife-blade, he said, 'How very noble of you! It's too bad I've already found myself another bride.'

'Another bride?' All the sparkle died from her face, making her look suddenly older and plain. 'Who?'

'I'm planning to marry Francesca, on the grounds that fair exchange is no robbery...'

It was a toss-up which of the two women was the most surprised.

'Though in this case I'm satisfied that I'm getting the best of the deal by far.'

Rallying a little, Melinda cried, 'I don't believe it. You're pulling my leg.'

When, his expression steely, he merely looked at her, she objected, 'But you've only known each other three days, and she's not your type at all.'

'I'm afraid you're wrong on both counts. Francesca and I met more than three years ago, and she's *exactly* my type.'

'But you said the rubies weren't the only thing you wanted back...'

'Nor are they. I'd like you to return my engagement ring.' Silently he held out his hand.

After hesitating for a second, Melinda reluctantly removed the ring and dropped it into his palm. Real venom in her tone, she snapped, 'I suppose you want it back so you can give it to *her*?'

'No,' Blaze answered evenly, 'I want it back because it happens to be another family heirloom. Francesca already has a ring.' Reaching for Fran's hand, he displayed the half-hoop of moonstones.

Refusing to look at it, Melinda begged, 'I need to talk to you alone. Please, darling. There's something I must tell you, something I want you to know...'

'Later, perhaps. First things first.'

Taking an object from his pocket, he tossed it across the

table to Kirk, who caught it in a reflex action. 'Just to even things up. You'll no doubt want that back.'

Fran realised it was her ring. So much had happened since Blaze had taken it from her finger that she hadn't given it a thought.

As Kirk stared down at the modest solitaire, Blaze suggested, 'Perhaps, while you're still a free man, you'd like to ask Melinda if she wants it?'

Then, his smile derisive, he added, 'Though I very much doubt if it's...shall we say...*princely* enough to make her change her mind.'

Fran looked from Kirk's hopeless face to Blaze's relentless one, and shivered. Judging by that, *'while you're still a free man'*, it seemed as though he did mean to call the police after all...

Unable to stand any more of his cat-and-mouse games, she rose to her feet.

Taking in her paleness, her air of quiet desperation, Blaze said, 'I still have several things to settle, but I asked the taxi to wait, so it might be as well if you go back now...'

Picking up her stole, he arranged it around her shoulders. 'I suggest you have a nice relaxing bath and get to bed early. Don't bother to wait up for me.'

Bending his head, his lips brushing her ear, he added, 'I don't want my bride to be too tired to enjoy her wedding night.'

Though his manner was intimate, his voice, Fran realised, had been pitched so that Melinda could hear.

Don't get mad, get even... Fran bit her lip.

A hand at her waist, he urged her towards the door. Leaving Melinda and Kirk sitting at the table, she went without a word. After all, what was there to say?

The window table was empty now, but the middle-aged couple who had occupied it earlier were standing in the lobby, looking at a range of leaflets giving details of shows and London attractions.

They turned and glanced at Blaze, who nodded silently before escorting Fran down the steps.

When they reached the street he lifted his hand, and the taxi, which had been waiting at the end of the cul-de-sac, drew up alongside the kerb.

Having put her into it, he produced one of the penthouse keys. 'You'll need this...' Then, handing the driver some notes, he directed, 'Back to the Empire Park, please.'

Before she could ask him what he planned to do, or how long he'd be, the door slammed and the taxi moved away.

During the journey back, Fran found herself replaying the unpleasant scene over and over again.

Shivering, she recalled Kirk's angry despair... Melinda's cold-blooded determination to ditch the man she had said she loved and end up on the winning side... Blaze's calculated cruelty...

She couldn't blame him for being angry, but she had been momentarily appalled by his ruthlessness, his decision to give no quarter...

When they reached the hotel, she thanked the driver and, stumbling out of the taxi, crossed the foyer to the lift.

She found the suite seemed depressingly silent and empty. Chilled and bone-weary, she decided to have a bath and go to bed, as Blaze had suggested.

But when she had donned her nightdress and crept beneath the duvet her troubled mind refused to let her sleep.

After almost an hour of restless tossing and turning, weary of her thoughts, she pulled on her robe, went into the elegant sitting room and, curling up on the settee, flicked on the TV.

The drama unfolding on the screen was tense and well-acted, but it failed to grip her, and after a few minutes she switched it off again.

Immediately her recalcitrant thoughts returned to what had happened earlier that evening.

Though Blaze had stated his intention of going through with the wedding, Fran felt unconvinced and anxious.

Her emotions, she realised, had tilted like a see-saw. At first she hadn't been able to bear the thought of marrying him when he didn't love her... Then she had reluctantly decided that though living with him would be painful, it would be better than living without him...

And now, when pride dictated that if he wanted another woman more she should step down, she couldn't bear the thought of losing him.

And it was on the cards that she would.

In spite of everything that had happened, Melinda had seemed very sure he still wanted her... And though he had denied loving her, it was obvious that, sexually at least, she had a powerful hold on him.

Perhaps his brush-off, his flaunting the fact that he had found himself another bride, had been intended simply to teach her a lesson?

Maybe when he was satisfied that she had been punished enough and was feeling suitably chastened he would agree to let bygones be bygones and take her back...?

Fran, her throat feeling as if it was full of shards of hot glass, swallowed hard. If he did, there was nothing she could do about it. Though he had said he wanted *her*, in truth she had only ever been second-best, a substitute for Melinda...

For what seemed like an age, while her thoughts continued to go round and round in circles and she grew steadily more miserable, she listened for his key in the lock.

When eleven-thirty came and went with still no sign of him she began to wonder desolately if perhaps he wasn't *coming* back.

Melinda had said she wanted to see him alone. That

could mean only one thing. She intended to use her sexual powers as a means of persuasion.

And she would no doubt find it easy.

Recalling the little scene in the Jacuzzi, Fran wished fervently that instead of being stupidly shy she had agreed to Blaze's suggestion.

Now it was too late, and if he was lying in Melinda's arms it was partly her own fault...

By the time another hour had dragged past all hope had gone, and the only thing she could feel was a leaden sense of despair. Three years ago she had lost the man she loved; now she had lost out again...

And this time she had lost so much more... The chance to be his wife, to have his children, to live with him for the rest of her life...

When he had said he only intended to marry once, that he wanted a happy and stable home for his family, she had never doubted that he meant it. And it was exactly what she herself wanted.

It was unlikely to be what *Melinda* wanted, but if Blaze was unable to see that for himself... How *could* a man with a brain as sharp as a Samurai sword be so *blind*?

Slow tears began to roll down her cheeks and, sniffing, she wiped them away with the back of her hand...

She was fast asleep when a touch wakened her. Opening heavy eyes, she looked up dazedly to find Blaze was sitting on the edge of the settee, gazing down at her.

His expression set and angry, he asked shortly, 'Why aren't you in bed?'

Sitting up, she pushed the tangle of ash-brown hair back from her flushed cheeks and said thickly, 'I couldn't settle...I kept wondering if...'

'If Varley had been carted off to gaol? Well, I can put your mind at rest. He hasn't been. At this precise moment he's at the airport, waiting to catch a flight to Rio de Janeiro.'

Unable to ask what she really wanted to know, she mumbled, 'Alone?'

'No. They patched up their differences, and Melinda is with him.'

All Fran could feel was joy, a deep and abiding gladness that Melinda and Kirk were gone and Blaze was here with her. Closing her eyes for an instant, she offered up a silent prayer of thanks.

'The fact that they're still together seems to have come as something of a shock to you,' Blaze observed coldly.

Her voice unsteady, she admitted, 'I *am* surprised. I felt quite sure she'd give Kirk up in favour of coming back to you.'

'So what did you have in mind? A *ménage à trois*?'

When she looked at him blankly, he added with a bite, 'Surely you haven't forgotten that I had made arrangements for *us* to be married tomorrow? Or should I say today?'

'No, of course I hadn't forgotten… But Melinda said she wanted to talk to you alone, and I…I thought she might have made you change your mind…'

A white line appearing round his mouth, he asked, 'Thought? Or *hoped*?'

She had started to shake her head when he said flatly, 'As it's turned two-thirty, and you look absolutely all-in, I suggest you get to bed.'

There were so many things he hadn't told her, so many questions left unanswered, but she felt dazed, unable to think straight. All she wanted to do was lie down with her head on Blaze's shoulder.

Making an effort, she struggled to her feet, but almost immediately swayed.

Stooping, Blaze lifted her and carried her through to her

bedroom. He set her on her feet by the bed and helped her off with her robe, before turning to leave.

'Blaze…' She barely breathed his name, but he paused and looked at her. 'Don't go. Please don't go.'

In the light that filtered in from the other room she saw him stiffen. 'I thought you wanted to sleep on your own tonight?'

'I've changed my mind.'

'In need of consolation?' he asked derisively. 'Well, why not?'

Fran gave a startled gasp as he caught the hem of her nightdress and, pulling it over her head, tossed it aside.

Turning back the duvet, he ordered, 'Get in.' Then, stripping off his own clothes, he slid in beside her.

She caught her breath, half wishing she hadn't begged him to stay. The winsome man who had teased her in the Jacuzzi was gone, in his place a hard-eyed, angry stranger.

'Something wrong?' he queried silkily.

'No,' she whispered.

'Then why are you looking so scared?'

'I—I'm not scared… Just tired.'

'Well, in that case we won't waste time on preliminaries.'

Always in the past he had been a tender, considerate lover, careful to see that her body was in tune with his. This time he made no attempt to arouse her, and when some hundred and sixty-odd pounds of bone and lean, hard muscle crushed down on her she tensed and tried to repulse him, upset and angry that he was treating her this way.

He caught her wrists and pinned them to the pillow, one each side of her head, while he made himself the master of her writhing body.

Perhaps her struggles triggered some switch, because suddenly, in spite of everything, she found herself responding.

He felt that response and began to move more slowly, coaxing and holding back, waiting until the core of tension had built to a climax and she gave a little gasping cry.

When he lifted himself away she lay quite still, engulfed in misery, struggling to hold back the tears that made her eyes ache and her cheeks feel stiff.

She had wanted *him*, the comfort of his arms and his presence; she had wanted him to hold her close while she fell asleep; she had wanted to pretend for just a little while that he loved her...

All he had offered her was cold-blooded sex, without a trace of kindness or caring.

Why had he stayed, if his only intention had been to cause her pain and humiliation? Was he regretting the fact that he had let Melinda go and taking it out on *her*...?

'Did I hurt you?'

The sudden urgent question broke into her unhappy thoughts, and she became aware that he was propped on one elbow looking down at her.

When she didn't immediately answer, he shook her a little. 'Did I? Francesca...answer me.'

'No.' At least not physically.

'Then why are you crying?'

'I'm not crying,' she mumbled.

That was manifestly untrue, and, clearly bothered, he pursued, 'I'm sorry I treated you so roughly. I must have been mad. I promise it won't ever happen again.'

'It's not that...'

'No, of course it isn't!' he said suddenly. His voice like ice, he added, 'I'm a fool not to have realised sooner...'

'Realised what?' she asked thickly.

'That in the circumstances I don't make a very satisfactory stand-in for Varley.'

She caught his arm. 'You're wrong...quite wrong... It's nothing like that...'

Brushing her hand away, he got out of bed.

'Please, Blaze, listen to me...'

Ignoring the choked plea, he gathered up his clothes, and a moment later the door closed quietly, but decisively, behind him.

Left alone in the big bed, Fran cried herself to sleep for the second time that night.

CHAPTER TEN

THE sound of a knock at the door awakened her, and Fran opened heavy eyes to find that sunshine was pouring through the light curtains and flooding the bedroom.

For a second or two her surroundings looked strange, and, dazed and disorientated, she couldn't remember where she was, or what she was doing here.

Then it all came back in a rush. She was at the Empire Park Hotel and this was her wedding day.

Unless, after what had happened the previous night, Blaze had changed his mind?

As the thought brought a swift stab of alarm there was another sharp rap, and almost immediately the door opened and Blaze walked in.

He had already showered and shaved. His dark hair was neatly brushed and he was dressed in a lightweight lounge suit.

'I'm sorry to have to wake you.' He sounded distantly polite. 'But it's almost nine-thirty. I've asked for breakfast to be sent up in about fifteen minutes.'

'I'll be ready.' She tried to match his tone.

Feeling vulnerable because of her nakedness, she waited until he'd gone before she got out of bed and hurried into the bathroom.

As quickly as possible she showered, and then, dressed in the only remaining clean undies in her case and a fawn jacket and skirt, went through to the sitting room.

The breakfast trolley had just arrived, and Blaze was standing by it pouring fresh orange juice. As soon as she'd taken her seat he sat down facing her, and, removing the silver lids from several dishes, asked, 'What will you have?'

Headachy and far from hungry, she was about to tell him that she only wanted coffee when, apparently reading her thoughts, he said firmly, 'You'll feel a great deal better if you have something to eat.'

Serving her with a piece of crisp bacon and a helping of scrambled eggs, he added, 'You had nothing last night, and I don't want you fainting at the altar.'

Swallowing a forkful of the light, fluffy eggs, she asked huskily, 'Then you haven't changed your mind? About the wedding, I mean?'

'No. Have you?' His narrowed grey eyes on her pale face, he added, 'After last night I couldn't blame you if you had.'

'No,' she said steadily, 'I haven't changed my mind.'

'Even though the threat of Varley ending up behind bars has been removed?'

'Was it ever a real threat?'

'What do you think?'

Buttering a slice of toast, she said incautiously, 'I rather doubt it.'

'But you still agreed to marry me?'

Ignoring that, she asked, 'What made you decide not to press charges?'

'For one thing, I detest publicity. If the story had got into the papers, which it almost certainly would have done, the media would have had a field-day. For another, my main concern was to get the necklace back. Once that was on the cards I could afford to be magnanimous.'

'You weren't showing any signs of magnanimity when I left the Royal George,' she said with feeling.

'At that point I wasn't feeling magnanimous. I was still angry enough to want to make both of them sweat a little.

In any case, it made sense to keep up the pressure until they returned the necklace.'

'As later on you let them leave for the airport, I presume they *have* returned it?'

By way of answer he pulled a thick brown paper envelope from his pocket and, opening the flap, poured the contents into his palm.

Fran drew a deep breath as the blood-red stones caught the light and flashed fire.

'You'll be able to wear it this afternoon,' he said, with a kind of bleak satisfaction.

She didn't care for her own sake, but as Blaze wanted to keep up the tradition she was only too delighted that he'd managed to recover it in time.

'Was it very difficult? Getting it back, I mean…?'

Dropping it into the envelope, he shook his head. 'The whole thing proved to be a great deal easier than I'd dared hope.'

'Only you were a long time coming home.'

He looked at her sharply.

Flushing a little, she said defensively, 'At least it *seemed* a long time.' With only partial truth, she added, 'I couldn't imagine what was keeping you.'

'There were a lot of things to be thrashed out before they started for the airport.'

'Oh.' She wondered what kind of things.

'If it hadn't been for that I would have got back a lot sooner. But of course it's swings and roundabouts… If they hadn't been planning to leave the country, they probably wouldn't have been carrying the necklace with them. The fact that they *were* saved a great deal of time and trouble.'

Thinking back to something Blaze had said the previous day, Fran asked, 'If you hadn't caught up with them, what were their chances of getting it safely through Customs?'

'Quite good, I think. Melinda was intending to throw it

in with the rest of her jewellery, most of which is artificial. If they'd gone to the trouble to look, the necklace is so over the top it's on the cards that anyone who wasn't an expert would have taken it for costume jewellery.

'It was a risk, of course, but there's one thing you can say for Melinda that you can't say for Varley: while she has few principles, she has plenty of guts.'

'There's something I don't understand,' Fran said in a rush. 'What made her decide to go with Kirk instead of...?' She broke off, biting her lip.

'Coming back to me?' he finished for her.

Remembering his reaction the previous night, her 'Yes' was barely above a whisper.

'You must take me for a fool if you think for one second that I would have *had* her back... A woman who's shown herself to be so completely hard and heartless...'

'But you...you seemed to *know* what she was like. You told me yourself that if you'd ever lost your money she would probably have left you...'

'I'd always been well aware that Melinda would put her own interests first, but I hadn't realised she could be *quite* so unscrupulous. I wish Varley joy of her...'

His mouth wry, he added, 'In spite of the fact that he deserves everything he gets, I could almost feel sorry for him.'

'There are two things I can't fathom,' Fran said slowly. 'The first is, what made her decide to stick with a man she'd called a penniless bankrupt...?'

Cynically, Blaze suggested, 'Perhaps, when I made it quite clear that I was no longer interested, she decided she loved him after all.' His lip curling, he added, 'I suppose any meal ticket's better than none.'

Reaching to fill Fran's coffee cup, he asked, 'What's the second?'

She finished her piece of toast and licked a sliver of

marmalade from her finger before replying, 'The thing that really puzzles me is why, when they have no money to start a new life, they're still going to South America?'

'Because I gave them an ultimatum,' Blaze said flatly. 'Either they left the country for good, or I'd turn them over to the police. It didn't take them long to decide that leaving the country was the better option.

'To be absolutely certain they got the message, I added that if they ever attempted to come back, I'd file charges against them. Just in case they tried to change their minds, I had them escorted to the airport by two of Ritters agents, who then waited to make sure they got on the plane.'

Two of Ritters agents... A sudden picture of the middle-aged couple who had been sitting close to the door in the Georgian Room flashed into her mind.

When he had escorted her out to the taxi, Blaze had nodded to them...

Watching her transparent face, he smiled mirthlessly. 'They look innocuous, don't they? That's why they're so good at their jobs.'

Seeing she'd finished her coffee, he put down his own empty cup and asked, 'Any more toast or anything?'

She shook her head. 'I've had a good breakfast.'

'Feeling better?'

'Much better. You were right about needing to eat.'

'Well, if you're ready...? You'll want some wedding finery, and at least the beginnings of a trousseau, so we ought to make a start.'

He rose to his feet, and, having pulled back her chair, picked up the envelope containing the necklace. 'But first I'd best put this away.'

Moving a Douglas Reed watercolour to reveal a small safe, he put the envelope inside and reset the code.

As they headed for the lift his hand at her waist was impersonal, his manner businesslike.

She felt a sudden painful longing for the man she had known and loved three years earlier—the warm, romantic man who would have held her hand and smiled at her.

It was sad to think that he had gone for ever, replaced by an aloof stranger who saw marriage merely as a business transaction.

As though to add weight to that thought, he observed distantly, 'It will probably be quicker to take a cab rather than get the car out. We need to be back here by three-fifteen at the latest, to give us both a chance to change.'

'Where…?' Her voice faltered and she tried again. 'Where are we getting married? You didn't say.'

'At All Saints.'

'Oh…' She was surprised. For some reason she'd presumed it would be at a register office rather than a church.

'It's at the bottom of Green Lane. We could see it from my old flat, if you remember?'

Yes, she remembered All Saints well. It was a small picturesque church with a tall, slender spire and a walled churchyard. On one side it was hemmed in by a high-rise apartment building, but on the other the Green Lane gardens gave it elbow room.

Coolly polite, he asked, 'I hope you don't mind being married in a church?'

'No, I prefer it.'

When they reached the main entrance, the doorman snapped to attention and asked, 'Taxi, Mr Balantyne?'

At Blaze's nod, he beckoned. The first vehicle in the queue pulled forward and he opened the door.

'Thank you, sir.' As they climbed in, he pocketed the generous tip.

'Knightsbridge, please,' Blaze instructed the driver, and a moment later they were on their way to one of the most famous departmental stores in the world.

The next few hours passed in a kind of whirl. When Fran

would have chosen with her usual caution, Blaze, who had his own ideas of what he wanted her to wear, would have none of it.

With no sign of embarrassment he selected a range of daring undies and some gossamer nightwear that brought a blush to Fran's cheeks.

Coats, dresses and suits came next, along with matching shoes and accessories.

Finally he hurried her up to the Bridal Department, saying, 'Now you need something to be married in.'

'Wouldn't one of the suits do?'

'Certainly not! I want my bride to look like a bride.'

Glancing along the racks of polythene-shrouded dresses, he selected an ivory wild silk with a fitted bodice, long, tight sleeves and a sweeping skirt.

'This one, if it fits,' he said decidedly.

It was beautiful, and unashamedly romantic, and Fran sighed as the saleslady pointed out a tiny bunch of blue forget-me-nots embroidered inside the hem.

As she was being led to one of the fitting rooms, Fran turned to Blaze a little hesitantly and asked, 'Do you want to see it on?'

'No,' he said almost curtly. 'Isn't it bad luck?'

The dress fitted like a dream.

Smiling, the saleslady hurried to fetch the matching shoes and headdress: a simple coronet with a veil as delicate as a spider's web.

When everything had been packed and dispatched to the hotel it was well after two, and Blaze insisted on them having a sandwich and a cup of tea before they started back.

By the time they reached the Empire Park it was almost a quarter past three. Waiting in their suite along with everything else was a florist's box. It contained a single off-white carnation and a bouquet of ivory freesias and deep red scented rosebuds.

Red roses for love…

'I hope you like it?' Unusually for him, Blaze sounded uncertain. 'As you'll be wearing the necklace, I thought your bouquet needed some colour.'

'It's beautiful,' she assured him tremulously.

'I'm sorry I can't provide you with a bridesmaid,' he went on, 'but if you need any help to get ready I'll ask the hotel to send up a maid.'

'No, thank you, I'm sure I can manage.'

Then, bearing in mind what he'd said about it being bad luck to see her in her dress, she asked, 'We won't be travelling to church together?'

'No, I'll be leaving first. A car will come for you about ten minutes to four.' As she turned away, he added, 'Oh, one more thing…the necklace… Before I go I'd like to put it on for you.'

She nodded. 'Yes, of course.' And hurried into the bathroom to shower and start to get ready.

Some fifteen minutes later there was a tap at the bedroom door. Hastily pulling on her robe, she went barefoot to answer it.

Blaze was standing outside wearing an immaculate pearl-grey suit, the carnation in his buttonhole.

He looked the epitome of the tall, dark and handsome bridegroom one read about in novels, Fran thought, with a strange feeling of unreality.

'Ready for this?' He held up the necklace.

'Yes.' She turned so that he could put it around her neck.

That done, he fastened the catch and allowed it to slip into place around her slender throat.

Turning back, she gazed up at him, waiting.

'It looks wonderful… Now you have everything. The

moonstone ring is old, the dress is new, the necklace is borrowed, and you have something blue.'

His words reminded her of the romantic man she had once known, and, her heart beating faster, she waited for his kiss.

But a moment later, without so much as a smile, he was gone, leaving her feeling empty and desolate.

Making an effort, she pulled herself together and went back to getting ready.

By a quarter to four she was fully dressed, her hair taken up into a smooth, silky knot, her coronet and veil in place.

Having changed her engagement ring to her right hand, she took one final look in the full-length mirror. The dress itself was every bride's dream. Lovely and enchanting, it almost managed to turn an ordinary girl into a fairy tale princess.

Though pale, in spite of careful make-up, and certainly no fairy tale princess, Fran was satisfied that she looked her best.

Not as stunning as Melinda would have looked, and nowhere near as sexy and exciting, but she would do her utmost to make Blaze a good wife, and no matter what happened she would never knowingly hurt him...

A knock at the outer door interrupted her thoughts. Realising it would be the car, she picked up her bouquet and hurried to open it.

To her surprise, Richard Henderson stood there, looking very personable in a smart grey suit, a carnation in his buttonhole.

'You look absolutely *beautiful*,' he told her. 'Edward's a very lucky man... And, speaking of Edward, I see he didn't warn you.'

'No, he didn't.' Feeling not quite so alone, she smiled at him. 'But I'm so glad you could come. I think you may well be our only guest.'

'Ah, but strictly speaking I'm not a guest. You see, Edward mentioned that you'd lost your father, and, knowing I was going to be in London this week, he asked if I could find time to give you away. Naturally I said I'd be only too pleased. You'll find I'm quite experienced,' he added, 'having given away two daughters of my own.'

Then, as she didn't speak, he asked a shade anxiously, 'I hope you don't mind?'

Swallowing the lump in her throat, she assured him, 'Of course I don't mind. In fact I'm *delighted*. To tell you the truth I was just starting to feel a little...overcome...'

'Then may I offer you an arm to lean on, or a shoulder to weep a few happy tears on? Whichever is the more appropriate.'

'An arm will do fine,' she told him, pulling her veil into place.

'In that case—' he presented a crooked elbow '—your carriage awaits you. A hackney carriage, admittedly, but it has a certain air about it.'

The 'certain air' proved to be white ribbons and flowers, and a smiling driver with a carnation in his buttonhole.

On the short journey to All Saints Fran found Richard's presence comforting and reassuring, though neither spoke, and silently thanked Blaze for having been thoughtful enough to arrange it.

The September day was a golden one, and they were bathed in sunshine as they walked up the paved path to the church door, where an elderly priest with a kind face was waiting to greet them.

Inside, though virtually empty of people, the church was full of flowers and incense and organ music. Sun shining through the stained glass windows made jewel-bright patterns along the backs of the polished pews and across the red carpet.

But, walking up the aisle on Richard's arm, Fran was

conscious of little but the man who was standing alone by the chancel steps.

Blaze turned at her approach, and just for an instant his face seemed to hold the look she'd always longed to see there. Then a shutter came down, and he was once again a cool and distant stranger.

As she took her place by his side the priest cleared his throat, and the short, simple service began.

Both made their responses quietly but clearly, Richard played his part with aplomb, and at the appropriate time Blaze produced two gold rings: one exquisitely chased, the other quite plain.

He slid the chased ring on to Fran's finger, and, though her hands were icy cold and not quite steady, she managed to put the thicker, heavier ring on to his finger without fumbling.

A few moments later they were declared man and wife, and the priest advised, 'You may kiss the bride.'

Blaze turned back her veil and, an expression in his eyes that she couldn't read, kissed her perfunctorily on the lips.

The two elderly ladies who had agreed to be witnesses, both smiling broadly and both dressed in their best, came forward to sign the register.

In no time the formalities were completed, and, after receiving everyone's congratulations and good wishes, the newlyweds said their thanks and walked down the aisle to Mendelssohn.

In the church porch, Blaze turned to Richard and asked, 'Have you time to join us for a glass of champagne?'

'I'm afraid not,' Richard said regretfully. 'I was due back in chambers ten minutes ago. But I'll make up for it when I come to Balantyne Hall.'

The two men shook hands.

'Please make it soon.' Fran kissed his cheek.

A moment later she and Blaze, enthusiastically showered

with rice by the two elderly ladies, were making for the waiting taxi.

Having helped her in, he gathered her skirt into a manageable pile before getting in beside her. They sat a good foot apart, and neither spoke on the journey back to the hotel, where the manager was waiting to wish them joy.

By the time Blaze had escorted her up to the penthouse, taking care neither to touch her nor look at her, Fran was feeling anything but joyful.

A quick peep at his face showed he looked scarcely any happier.

As though aware of her glance, he asked abruptly, 'What would you like to do? Stay here the night or go home?'

Unusually for him, he seemed tense and restless, and she wondered what to say for the best.

Making up her mind, she answered, 'Go home,' and saw by his expression that she'd made the right choice.

'Then as soon as you've changed I'll have everything put in the car and we'll get off.'

'You'll want this.' She fumbled to unfasten the necklace.

He shook his head. 'Leave it on. It'll be safer that way. Tomorrow I'll make arrangements to have it returned to the bank.'

Within ten minutes of her taking off her wedding finery and putting on a stone-coloured silk suit they were on their way.

Tired, and emotionally exhausted, she dozed on and off for most of the journey to Balantyne Hall, only waking fully as they drew up outside.

They were scarcely out of the car when the door opened and the butler appeared.

'Have everything brought in and the car put away, will you?' Blaze instructed tersely.

'Certainly, sir.' Then, with due deference, 'May I, on

behalf of myself and the staff, wish you and madam every happiness.'

Blaze merely nodded, while Fran managed a smile and, 'Thank you, Mortimer.'

The butler cleared his throat. 'What time will madam require dinner?'

Flustered at being referred to, Fran glanced at Blaze. Getting no help from him, she answered as steadily as possible, 'The usual time, please, Mortimer.'

Decisively, Blaze added, 'Please tell Cook to keep it light, and we'll eat upstairs in preference to the dining room.'

The butler bowed, and moved sedately away to do his master's bidding.

Looking like a pair of distant strangers, rather than newlyweds, Fran and Blaze made their way upstairs in silence.

Showing he'd given his permission for the suite to be cleaned, everywhere gleamed with elbow grease and polish, and there was a large bowl of fresh flowers on the bureau.

Though a fire burned cheerfully in the big grate, the evening air coming through the open windows made the room decidedly cool.

But no cooler than the atmosphere between Blaze and herself, Fran thought, her spirits at rock-bottom.

She shivered, and apparently in response to that involuntary movement he went to close the windows. Then, his back to the room, he stood staring out.

There was a discreet tap at the door.

When Blaze neither moved nor spoke, Fran went to open it.

Hannah and two of the menservants were outside, their arms full of the morning's shopping. 'Where would you like it all put, miss...I mean, madam...?' the maid asked.

Fran glanced across at Blaze for guidance, but, still staring out of the window, he appeared oblivious.

The previous night he had made it plain that he intended them to share a room, but in the face of his present coldness she hesitated to invade his privacy.

Coming to a decision, she said, 'In here, please,' and led the way to what had been Melinda's room. 'You can leave it all on the bed.'

The various boxes and packages duly deposited, the maid asked, 'Would you like me to put everything away for you, madam?'

Needing something to occupy her, Fran answered, 'No, thank you, Hannah. I'll do it myself.'

As soon as the door had closed behind the servants, with a heavy heart she began to hang her new clothes in the now empty wardrobe.

When she got to the wedding dress she had a job to hold back the tears. It seemed only too clear that, almost before the ceremony was over, Blaze had been having second thoughts.

But *why*? What had she done to make him change his mind?

Everything put away, and the room tidy once more, she stood irresolute. Now what was she to do? How was she to get through the remaining minutes and hours of the day, alone with a man who was virtually ignoring her existence?

Well, if he was going to treat her that way, she thought with a sudden determination, at least she was entitled to know why.

Chin high, she marched back into the living room to find that Blaze had removed his jacket and was sitting in his shirt-sleeves, staring morosely into the fire.

She sat down opposite, and, taking her courage in both hands, said quietly, 'I'd like to know what I've done?'

He lifted his head and looked at her. 'Done? *You* haven't done anything.'

'Then what's wrong?'

Heavily, he said, 'Marrying you was a mistake…'

Feeling as though she was mortally wounded, she stared at him.

After a moment, his face full of self-disgust, he went on, 'If I hadn't been so damned selfish, things might have worked out for you.'

'I—I don't know what you mean.'

'Though I'm certain Varley only meant to *use* you, after the way Melinda treated him he would have been mad not to have appreciated a woman who loved him and would have stuck by him. Along with loyalty and integrity you have a lot of spirit, and if I'd let well alone you might have made a go of things. But I couldn't bear to think of you going back to him.'

As Fran began to shake her head, he said, 'You asked why Melinda decided to stick with him… It was because I paid her to. You asked why they left for South America… It was because I agreed to take care of all Varley's debts and provide them with enough capital to start a new life… If they stayed *together*.'

Dazedly, she said, 'You did all that to stop me going back to him?'

'I knew that in spite of everything you wanted to.'

'But I didn't—'

'There's no point in denying it. You were hoping I'd take Melinda back so it would leave Varley free for you.'

'You're quite wrong.'

'I don't think so. When Varley said Melinda had never intended to have my children you knew it was the truth, I could see by your face. But you kept quiet.'

'Only because I thought you *wanted* her back. And you had been warned—'

'And when I hinted that Varley might end up in gaol you were so upset I thought you were going to faint…'

'I couldn't stand you being so deliberately cruel—'

'Then later, when I got back to the hotel I could see you'd been crying over him—'

'It wasn't *him* I'd been crying over—'

As though she hadn't spoken, he went on, 'That's what made me so angry... Why I treated you the way I did... I'm sorry about that...'

He rubbed a hand over his eyes, as though to erase the disturbing memory.

'And I'm sorry I forced you to marry me. I tried to tell myself that on some level you *wanted* to, but if I'd been honest I would have admitted it was only sexual attraction.'

'But it wasn't just sexual attraction.'

Disregarding her denial, he said bleakly, 'I shouldn't have been blaming you for still loving him. I'm only too aware that no one can stop loving to order... God knows I've tried.'

She knew he'd once loved someone, because when she'd asked, 'Then you've never been in love?' he'd answered, 'Oh, yes, I have.' Now, watching the naked pain on his face, her heart bled for him.

There was a long pause before he went on, 'After Sherrye had staged her coup, I did my utmost to find you. When I was unsuccessful, I tried to put you out of my mind, tried to stop loving you... That's the reason I gave up my flat. It held too many memories...'

So it was *her* he'd loved... Warmth spread through her, bringing fresh life and dispelling all the previous desolation.

'Then, when I'd abandoned all hope,' Blaze went on, 'you suddenly came back into my life. I tried to tell myself that I no longer cared. All my plans were made. Everything was cut and dried. But I took one look at you and I knew my feelings hadn't changed...'

Hands clasped together, she stayed motionless while gladness bubbled inside like a fountain of pure joy.

'Only it wasn't that simple... I could no doubt have paid Melinda off, but you were in love with your fiancé... That's why I was pleased when Melinda and Varley ran off together. I told myself that he was no good, and you'd soon stop loving him. I convinced myself that I could make you love me.

'It wasn't until the ring was on your finger and it was too late that I realised I'd only been fooling myself. A marriage where neither partner loves the other has a fair chance of success, but one-sided loving seldom works.'

'I'm forced to agree with you,' she said.

He sighed deeply. 'If you want an annulment...?'

'Why should I want an annulment?'

'You've just agreed that one-sided loving is unlikely to work.'

'Who said anything about *our* loving being one-sided? If you'd *listen* to me for a change, instead of *telling* me...'

The grey eyes so dark they looked almost black, he stared at her.

'I loved you three years ago, that's why I couldn't bear to stay, and I love you still. There's never been anyone else but you.'

As, his face alight with hope, he opened his mouth to speak, she said severely, 'Will you please not interrupt? For a while I *thought* I loved Kirk. But that night you carried me up to my room and I kissed you I knew it was *you* I loved, and I could never marry Kirk. What little feeling there was between us had been all on my side, a kind of infatuation.' Without bitterness, she added, 'An infatuation he made use of for his own ends.'

Seeing the way Blaze's jaw tightened, she said hastily, 'No, I don't mean in *that* way. When I told you we were sleeping together, it wasn't the truth. The night we got engaged I'd almost *expected* him to want to take me to bed. But he drove me home and kissed me goodnight without even coming in... Of course, though I didn't know it then, he had Melinda.'

Hoarsely, Blaze demanded, 'If you've never been to bed with him, why did you lie about it?'

'Just at that minute I was angry with you for making fun of him...'

Suddenly Blaze was on his feet. Gripping her upper arms, he hauled her out of her chair. 'I could cheerfully turn you over my knee and spank you... If you knew how much torment that lie has cost me. I was so damned jealous that every time I thought of him touching you I felt like breaking his neck.'

Looking up at Blaze through long lashes, she said demurely, 'Well, if we're staying together, I hope you're not going to turn into a wife-beater?'

'I'll probably be able to come up with some other way of keeping you under control.'

'Such as?'

'Well, there's one that springs to mind. I'll no doubt be able to think of more while we're on our honeymoon.'

'Are we having a honeymoon?'

'We certainly are. A honeymoon that starts with a month in Hawaii and, I'm prepared to bet, will last for the rest of our lives.'

'I won't argue with that,' she said pertly. 'But I have one question. When does this honeymoon start?'

'When would you like it to start?'

'There's no time like the present.'

As he glanced towards the bedroom, she shook her head. 'I'm in no mood to be conventional.'

He raised a quizzical brow. 'What mood *are* you in?'

'Adventurous...that is, for *me*...'

Leaning against him, and punctuating the words with teasing baby kisses, she suggested, 'I'd like you to make love to me in front of the fire, while I'm still wearing the Balantyne rubies.'

'Brilliant thinking, my heart's darling.'

He caught her roving lips and kissed her deeply, making her body melt and her toes curl, before adding, 'I'd hoped to keep up the Ballantyne family traditions, but I hadn't expected to be starting a new one.'

Getting down to business in the boardroom... and the bedroom!

A secret romance, a forbidden affair, a thrilling attraction…

What happens when two people work together and simply can't help falling in love—no matter how hard they try to resist?

Find out in our new series of stories set against working backgrounds.

Look out for

THE MISTRESS CONTRACT
by Helen Brooks, Harlequin Presents® #2153
Available January 2001

and don't miss

SEDUCED BY THE BOSS
by Sharon Kendrick, Harlequin Presents® #2173
Available April 2001

Available wherever Harlequin books are sold.

HARLEQUIN®
Makes any time special ™

VIVA LA VIDA DE AMOR!

They speak the language of passion.

In Harlequin Presents®, you'll find a special kind of lover—full of Latin charm. Whether he's relaxing in denims or dressed for dinner, giving you diamonds or simply sweet dreams, he's got spirit, style and sex appeal!

Latin Lovers is the new miniseries from Harlequin Presents® for anyone who enjoys hot romance!

Meet gorgeous Antonio Scarlatti in
THE BLACKMAILED BRIDEGROOM
by Miranda Lee, Harlequin Presents® #2151
available January 2001

And don't miss sexy Niccolo Dominici in
THE ITALIAN GROOM
by Jane Porter, Harlequin Presents® #2168
available March 2001!

Available wherever Harlequin books are sold.

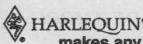

HARLEQUIN®
makes any time special—online...

eHARLEQUIN.com

your romantic
books

♥ **Shop online!** Visit Shop eHarlequin and discover a wide selection of new releases and classic favorites at great discounted prices.

♥ **Read** our daily and weekly Internet exclusive serials, and participate in our interactive novel in the reading room.

♥ **Ever dreamed of being a writer?** Enter your chapter for a chance to become a featured author in our Writing Round Robin novel.

• • • • •

your romantic
life

♥ **Check out** our feature articles on dating, flirting and other important romance topics and get your daily love dose with tips on how to keep the romance alive every day.

• • • • • •

your
community

♥ **Have a Heart-to-Heart** with other members about the latest books and meet your favorite authors.

♥ **Discuss** your romantic dilemma in the Tales from the Heart message board.

your romantic
escapes

♥ **Learn** what the stars have in store for you with our daily Passionscopes and weekly Erotiscopes.

♥ **Get the latest scoop** on your favorite royals in Royal Romance.

If you enjoyed what you just read,
then we've got an offer you can't resist!

Take 2 bestselling love stories FREE!

Plus get a FREE surprise gift!